Twice Upon a Time

*Faery tales
with a dash of modern magic*

Decadent Publishing Company, LLC
P.O. Box 407
Klawock, AK 99925
www.decadentpublishing.com

Twice Upon a Time
All Rights Reserved/January 2011
Cover design by Sahara Kelly and Scott Carpenter
ISBN: 978-1-936394-68-5

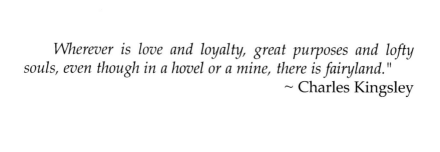
Wherever is love and loyalty, great purposes and lofty souls, even though in a hovel or a mine, there is fairyland."
~ Charles Kingsley

In late 2010, while at a booksigning and doing what she loves best—meeting her reader fans—author Tina Gerow was struck with symptoms of a dangerous medical condition known as Arteriovenous Malformation. What followed was a series of operations, a lengthy hospital stay and rehabilitation. We are happy to report that Tina is doing well, though her complete recovery is an ongoing process. In cases like this, medical expenses can mount rapidly and, as it often does, the literary community steps in to help however they can. This book is the result of an outpouring of just a few of Tina's friends from the Romantic Times Faery Court.

With the encouragement and generosity of Lisa Omstead at Decadent Publishing, (also a sister fae from the Court), who stated "let's do this" without hesitation, the stories were gathered and the cover art willingly donated. Lisa and her editors worked tirelessly and with consummate professionalism to compile these stories into a "faery special" anthology of modern faery tales which we call "Twice Upon a Time ~ faery tales with a dash of modern magic! " You may recognize them, of course, but they're not exactly the way you remember...

This one-of-a-kind anthology includes the literary talents of Eden Robins, Amanda McIntyre, Sahara Kelly, Taige Crenshaw, Vijaya Schartz, Janet Miller, Joy Nash, Liddy Midnight and Kayce Lassiter...and a contribution from you— the buyer of this book! Every author is donating 100% of their royalties to the fund established to assist Tina with her medical bills.

My thanks to my sister fae, gifted and giving people, as well as authors, who stepped up to put this anthology together for Tina's benefit. Thanks also to Lisa, Heather and their staff at Decadent Publishing who made it a reality. To you, for buying this book and spreading the love of the fae with your purchase. And to Tina, whose lovely, tenacious spirit continues to inspire us.

~ Amanda McIntyre

Learn more about Arteriovenous Malformation:
http://www.ninds.nih.gov/disorders/avms/avms.htm

Tina's benefit website:
https://sites.google.com/site/tinagerowandfamily/

Romantic Times BOOKlovers convention:
http://www.rtconvention.com

So What is this Faery Ball Business All About?

(A look behind the scenes at the event of the season, as reported by veteran Fae Sahara Kelly!)

Once upon a time...

There was a wonderful magazine created for readers who enjoyed romance novels. It was called, appropriately enough, Romantic Times BOOKlovers Magazine. The brainchild of a wonderful lady named Kathryn Falk, the magazine appealed to everyone who had ever enjoyed a romance. Before long, those readers were clamoring for more, something they could really get their teeth into. Something that would give them even more personal contact with the literary world they embraced on a regular basis.

Hence the birth of the Romantic Times Convention, known to its aficionados as "RT". Every year, in a different city, readers, writers and other industry professionals gather for five days devoted to all things literary. RT has grown through the more than twenty-five years of its existence to include other genres—Young Adult, Mysteries, Urban Fantasies and so on, no longer restricting itself to the still-beloved world of romance novels. For those of us who are part of this literary universe, the RT Convention has become a yearly treat to ourselves, sort of a combination Super Bowl, World Series and Stanley Cup event for everyone who loves a good novel. It's a chance to mingle with those who write, those who read and those who publish.

During the Convention there are the usual assorted panels, seminars, teas, gatherings and so on. But in the evenings there are special gala events, designed for all attendees. Parties where the music invites dancing, the laughter can be heard over the beat from the loudspeakers and everyone has the chance to mingle en masse. Most often in costume, depending on the theme of the particular party. So many of us still quietly nurture that "dress-up" gene, the hidden facet of our personalities that takes wing when draped in chiffon, sprinkled with glitter, or painted from head to toe in rainbow shades of tulle. Costumes are a traditional part of the RT experience and can range from the impromptu—"pass me that sheet…"—to the incredibly ornate— "Didn't I see that gown in that historical special on TV last week?" As you can see from all this fun information, attendees at RT conventions have the time of their lives, moving from a panel hosted by their favorite author to a party where they can dress up as a vampire and not worry about their kids being scarred for life as Mom goes out on the dance floor and swings her way through "Achy Breaky Heart" with twenty other vampires.

This, then, is the environment that gave rise to the initial concept of the RT Faery Ball.

Way back in 2005, best-selling author Cheyenne McCray and her friend, award-winning writer, Eden Robins were appointed to the role of Queens for the very first Faery Ball event. Cheyenne and Eden recruited some of their fellow authors, inviting them to join what would become known as "The Faery Court". Many writers, this author included, leaped at the opportunity to swan around a fancy hotel wearing fairy-like apparel, since it wasn't anything we did on a regular basis. At least not in my neck of the woods.

The first Romantic Times Faery Court Ball was held in Daytona in 2006, and to say it was a success is an understatement. Eager to sample the newest evening party, guests filled the ballroom and more tables were needed to accommodate the overflow. Behind the scenes, we nervous Fae gathered for photographs in a suite a few floors above the beach. We were prodded, pushed, posed—moved around a little and balanced on chairs that seemed much too fragile to hold us. With the background of the evening light on the Atlantic Ocean, the first Faeries made their debut and to this day the resulting photo evokes wonderful memories of that very special evening.

To maintain as much of the secrecy surrounding the Faeries as possible, we are usually shepherded from our gathering place to an undisclosed location in the ballroom where we can be revealed in all our glory to the "oohs" and "aahs" of the audience. Most of whom politely refrain from laughing. We do appreciate that, by the way, thank you.

In Daytona, for example, getting to the ballroom was an adventure in and of itself, since we took the back way to the event. In most hotels, the back way isn't something guests usually see. It involves freight elevators, kitchens, small dark passageways lined with crates and more kitchens lined with rolling carts holding salads. It requires walking carefully over wires and cables and other things on the floor while wearing high heels that almost always pinch. It demands a maximum of four Faeries in an elevator that can hold twelve people. The reason being that Faeries have wings, some of 'em large enough to achieve lift-off in a strong breeze. And it involves a large number of hotel employees who probably thought they'd seen everything until a batch of winged and sparkling wonders invaded their domain shedding glitter and wisecracks. Fortunately, since Faeries seem to develop a tendency to giggle and smile once in costume, the employees—after their initial shock—laugh back, untangle wings from elevator machinery and generally help out where they can, rescuing Faeries who have strayed from the herd and pointing them in the right direction. You can bet it's good for dinner table conversation later when they get home.

The ball in Daytona held everything one would expect…sparkling lights, flowers, trees…and a small elegant dance floor where the Faeries executed a sort of Maypole dance featuring a cover model. It was here, during this first Faery Ball, that we realized just because we can write novels doesn't mean we're good at learning dances. Mishaps notwithstanding, all had a wonderful evening and the stage was set for the incorporation of the Faery Ball into the RT Convention schedule on an annual basis.

Many of us returned the following year, again under the leadership of Cheyenne and Eden who would continue to reign over the court for five years. We decided that it was time to develop a "theme" for the Ball. This would help focus our decorative efforts into one area and also be useful to those who wished to wear an appropriate costume. Guests began to enter into the Faery spirit, creating fabulous outfits for themselves, scouring shops for wings, and the Fae responded by including a costume competition during the event—something that is now eagerly anticipated by our guests. The creativity of people when given a theme is boundless...we have been amazed and astounded over the years by some of the incredible outfits. Everything from white peacock feathers to cotton balls, imitation horses' hooves and more face paint than Ringling Brothers could use in a year. For those involved, they will tell you that the costume competition at the Faery Ball is as much a part of the evening as the dinner and dancing.

In Houston 2007, came the Medevial Faery Court Ball where a wonderful set was created, that resembled the jousting field with the Fae seated either side of the stage like nobles watching the action. Yes, we referred to it as Fae-in-a-Box. Or having received a five-minute penalty for illegal use of wings. There are all kinds of humor, jokes when wearing wings and a Faery costume tend toward the less complex, but are no less funny. Although it helps to be there at the time. The Medieval ball challenged us with the task of getting elaborate gowns up a tiny backstage staircase, and the following year—2008 in Pittsburgh—we dove UNDER THE SEA and learned that being lined up alphabetically might not always work for writers, even though we're supposed to know which letters come before others.

Heading back to Florida in 2009, we opted to explore the concepts of light and dark for our theme, so guests were invited to choose either the SEELIE AND THE UNSEELIE fae as their allegiance.

Then came Columbus for the 2010 RT Faery Ball where the theme was ELEMENTAL aspects - earth, water, air and fire. It was a wonderful, though bitter-sweet, experience. It was on this night that the court bid farewell to the two Queens who had steered the event to the success it currently enjoys. Cheyenne McCray and Eden Robins have earned the eternal thanks of the hundreds of people who have enjoyed the Balls over the first five years, and the Faeries who have looked to them for advice, guidance and inspiration. Now wearing the title of "Fae Emeritii", Cheyenne and Eden will always be a part of the Faery Court, in our hearts if not in person.

As it is for all the fae who have and will continue to host this special event, we truly believe that, "Once a fae, always a fae."

Many of the current Fae were there in Daytona the first time wings rippled in the breeze. Your correspondent is one, along with Amanda McIntyre, another Fae who has served in each Court. Together we have accepted the Queens' mantle from Cheyenne and Eden and will be overseeing the fun for 2011 and 2012. At that point we will pass the Wands of Office to two new Queens.

The camaraderie engendered by being part of the Faery Court is hard to explain. Initially, contact is by Internet Group postings, sharing ideas, looking for costume suggestions, clarifying some minor point or other and generally indulging in the occasional comment or question about the whole Faery deal. We welcome new Fae and bid farewell to those not joining the new Court.

Many of us have already met, some we know by their work, others we've not met at all and look forward to doing so. Traditionally we host a contest during the months before the convention, offering gifts to the lucky winners and encouraging folks who are planning on attending to remember the Faery Ball.

Each year a new element is added to this spectacular event. In the past two years we've added a "Faery Bling" auction which goes to benefit literacy programs in the host city of the convention. In 2011, we will premiere the print version of this book and have it available for sale at the RT Faery Ball and all week in the Club RT.

So you might be wondering why on earth I'm telling you

all this stuff. Well, you're reading this because the writers who have contributed to this anthology have joined with the publisher in expressing a hope that you will begin to understand the nature of this event and those who are involved in it. We hope that from these lighthearted musings you will be able to sense the deep commitment we Faery Courtiers feel about the Faery Ball and each other, and begin to understand that being a Faery for the RT Convention doesn't end at the stroke of midnight.

With luck, you can see from these brief vignettes some of the laughter and adventures shared by the Court. Some of the delightful memories that will remain with us no matter where life takes us. And you might perhaps be able to understand the nature of the friendships formed while traversing so many of the rather strange but entertaining moments as a member of the Faery Court.

It is this friendship, a uniting bond, which has brought us together in support of our Sister Fae Tina Gerow. And this friendship which has led, ultimately, to the book you are now reading. Many of us feel that being a member of the RT Faery Court touches our lives with a little extraordinary magic, for such is true friendship.

It is our sincerest wish that each and every one of our readers will be touched by that same magic.

Blessings be,
Sahara Kelly

❦ Contents ❧

The Prince and the Pea

Amanda McIntyre

Once upon a time there was a young executive. Her name was Rosa O'Flannery, named after her Irish grandmother and her Hispanic grandmother. She was very bright and her skill and determination had taken her far up the corporate ladder in the successful industry of advertising.

She'd become the only female officer on the board of 'Sweet Slumber Mattress' by being self-sufficient, independent, and working night and day not concerned whether she might ever find her 'Prince Charming.' Who had time for that? Certainly not her, she didn't have time for such trivialities…not when her boss and half the board of directors constantly kept their beady, ancient eyes on her. Ancient all, except for one and Gerald, well, Gerald didn't count. He was the resident geek—personified.

Rosa's cell phone vibrated against her hip, startling her in the middle of her ten o'clock meeting with the all-male board. She smiled contritely at her boss, who paused momentarily in the midst of his ten-minute dissertation on bedspring quality. Mentally she wished whoever was on the other end of the phone would dissipate in a puff of smoke. Rosa tugged the cell phone from her suit pocket and frowned at the unknown number flashing on the tiny screen. She sighed and snapped the lid shut to disconnect the annoying caller. No sooner had she tucked it back in her pocket however when it began to buzz again, vibrating like an angry bee against her hip.

Gerald Hopper, junior associate for 'Sweet Slumber'

slanted a side look at her over the top of his thick black-rimmed glasses. Though he was likely (to her best guess, and not that she noticed) close to her age, Gerald had a penchant for dressing at least thirty years in the past. Perhaps he thought it gave him greater credibility with the aging board members, but to Rosa it was plain annoying.

In the mattress business, Rosa had never thought about being the only female on the board. She felt she'd risen above the testosterone and as such earned the nickname 'Princess' among her fellow board members. Rosa had learned to grit her teeth and smile when the name was used, but it only fueled the belief that she was more than capable and uniquely qualified to 'reign' over this tribe of aging misfits.

Granted, maybe that was the reason she didn't feel that she needed a man in her life. She already had more men than she could handle; well, except for the sex, which she chose to put out of her mind entirely—mostly.

To add to the frustration, however, she was none too happy when she was passed over by the board and instead Gerald received the Junior Associate position. Fortunately, he hadn't let it go to his head, geeky as it was.

"Sorry, wrong number," she whispered as she leaned close to Gerald. Rosa offered a weak smile.

Sensing his frosty gaze, she purposely averted her eyes from her boss.

"Ms. O'Flannery, is there something you wish to address with the rest of this board?" he spoke in a condescending tone. Big surprise there.

Her gaze snapped up and she found eleven sets of eyes fixed upon her—if one didn't take into account Mr. Higgenfield's glass eye that was forever straying in the opposite direction.

"Sorry sir, wrong number. I apologize." She again pressed the off button on her phone and shoved it back into her pocket.

Her boss cleared his throat. "I don't need to tell you people how crucial this new ad campaign is to our sales. It's vital we come up with a strategy that will knock the sheets off our competition. You have exactly twenty-four hours to come up with a brilliant market plan for our new 'Royalty Slumber' line. Now get busy and I want every idea on this table no later than ten a.m. tomorrow morning. Don't be late."

His stern gaze fell on Rosa and she lowered her eyes to the table.

"I leave my phone at my desk," Gerald whispered to her as they shuffled like livestock from the boardroom.

The hairs on Rosa's neck bristled with awareness of his mouth near her earlobe. "Thanks, I'll remember that next time." Mentally she took his horn-rimmed glasses and twisted them into small pieces.

Oblivious, Gerald tucked his file under his arm and retrieved his day-planner, perusing its pages with the giddiness of a child with a new toy. "Okie dokie, Princess, what are you doing *today* for lunch?" He pushed his geeky glasses up the bridge of his nose.

For a split second, she imagined he wore form-fitting blue tights beneath his out-of-style business suit. There was potential that given a massive makeover and a few lessons in social skills, that Gerald *could* be attractive. The operative word, of course, being *could*. If he would tone down the whole 'Clark Kent' image just a hair. Moreover, speaking of that, why did he feel the need to plaster down his gorgeous raven locks with tons of gel? Maybe it was to prevent flyaways. Rosa held the grin that threatened to lead to disaster if she allowed him to see it. After all, in all likelihood, the way things were going, Gerald could one day be her boss.

Rosa shuddered, yet kept her smile congenial. "I'm sorry. I have a ton of paperwork to weed through." She checked her watch to be sure she didn't miss the mail carrier's next round at ten seventeen on the dot.

"Again? You know, Rosa, its not good to skip meals. It lessens the vital nutrients needed to produce brain cells, and without those, well then you can't very well think of the perfect ad campaign, can you?"

He gave her a grin that exuded his self-brilliance.

She held his geek-personified gaze a moment not wanting to hurt him, yet once again reminding herself that if *this* was the only nibble she ever got from a man (and that was using the term loosely) then she'd just as soon starve. Still, when he screwed up his face like a grumpy ten-year-old who didn't get his way, it produced the most adorable little dimple at the corner of his mouth. A mouth that in the right setting just might have potential.

Never mind that.

"I have an absolute mountain of work. I'd planned to grab something from the break room and eat while I go through it. I'm sorry Gerald, maybe another time?" She forced her gaze from his mouth and back to the hazel eyes blinking at her from behind those thick lenses. There were moments, though rare, when she wanted to immerse herself in their depth. She shook her head from her ridiculous thoughts. "It's been great talking to you, Gerald, but I've got to run. Time waits for no man, or woman." She smiled as she walked between the shoulder high cubicle walls.

"And all work and no play makes Princess a dull...uh, girl, er...woman," he called after her. Sure, it was meant to be funny, but she couldn't help but feel the ill-timed jab as several co-workers turned to look up at her as she passed by.

She waved her hand in dismissal, keeping her chin high and her smile as bright as possible. Who had time to play anyway? Maybe Gerald did, but not her. If the powers-that-be wanted a kickass advertising campaign, then by golly they were going to get one they couldn't refuse. She would show that board that she was more than a Princess; she was a passionate force to be reckoned with.

Gerald watched the defiant flounce of her skirt as she walked away. He admired her grit against the geezers still running the company. His façade of dressing down was meant to satisfy their egos, in hope that they would listen to his ideas. The administrative heads of *Sweet Slumber* were a bit behind the times, make that atrociously behind the times, when it came to selling their products. When other companies appealed to the bright, youthful zesty ads to instill a sense of passion into the customers, *Sweet Slumber* instead held the concept that everyone who purchased their product was geriatric and therefore no longer interested in passion in bed.

Gerald hoped that slowly but surely, he could change their minds with a campaign that would appeal to Ms. O'Flannery as well. He'd been trying to get a date with her for months, but when the 'Princess' made up her mind on something there was little else that changed it. He wondered why she stayed, when it seemed the elder board members sometimes handled her like a child.

His attention snapped back to Prin—Rosa, as she stopped to sign off a chart for her secretary. She gave the woman a carefree laugh and flipped her dark hair over her shoulder. Gerald had dreamt of how her silky hair would feel between his fingers, had thought of it for months in his private fantasies. With a final glance over her shoulder, she offered him a barely perceptible smile and closed her office door.

At home that night, Rosa chewed on her charcoal pencil, her over-sized artist pad propped up in her lap. The pages were still blank. She'd been staring at it for over an hour wishing an idea to materialize. Her television was turned on, mainly out of habit, but she'd snapped off the volume hoping to jar her creativity. On the screen played an old black and white movie that she stared at from time to time, waiting for them to turn to her and give her a brilliant campaign ad. In his usual spot at the end of her couch, her blonde tabby lay curled in a fuzzy ball, oblivious to her plight. An empty pint of *'Chunky Monkey'* and a crumpled bag of potato chips lay on the coffee table, evidence of her frustration and supper rolled into one. Tomorrow she silently promised she'd walk the treadmill for an extra fifteen minutes over her lunch break.

Rosa's thoughts drifted back to the television screen. At this rate, she'd need the exercise to clear out the frustration of being muscled out again by Gerald. A laugh escaped her mouth, startling the cat's slumber. He peered at her with one sleepy eye, stretched, and went back to sleep. As if Gerald possessed a single passionate thought in his body, which was too bad, since despite his universal geeky side, his body was screaming off the charts in terms of seriously *fine*.

"I don't suppose you've considered the fact that you barely spend any time at all on a mattress?"

Rosa blinked a couple of times, her focus aimed at the characters on the television. At first, she thought the woman on the screen was a kind-looking elderly lady touting the comfort of a new product.

As Rosa watched however, it seemed the woman was looking directly at her.

She picked up the remote and changed the channel. Perhaps the stress was causing her to hallucinate and a nap would be a good idea to refresh her before she plodded on.

"You already work too much, you don't eat the right foods, and you never go out just to have fun." The old woman's eyes were dazzling blue. "I'm not sure you understand what passion is truly all about. There is such thing as having a passion for life, that can be as important."

Rosa was dreaming, of course that was it. She reached down, grabbed a hunk of her flesh, and pinched hard. "Ow."

"Rosa my dear, you aren't dreaming and I am not a figment of your imagination, though I will say that you could use a little help in that department."

"Right." Rosa laughed as she snapped the off button of her remote. The screen went black. She tossed the silver box on the table and reached for the chips. Her hand hung in mid air as once more she heard the voice.

"You tried that this morning when I attempted to reach you on your cell phone."

The old woman's image magically appeared again on the television screen.

Rosa grabbed her cat and clutched the yowling animal to her. Surely, there was a glitch in her remote, how else could she possibly explain this?

"What, are you going to do, launch him at me like a catapult?" Her nasal laughter ended in an unlady-like snort. "Get it...cat-a-pult?" Her laughter died to a trickle. "Sorry, I crack myself up sometimes."

"Who are you, and what do you want?"

"Aha, now we're getting somewhere. I hate having to appear in bathroom mirrors and cereal bowls, but you do what you have to do to get a client's attention." The old woman shrugged.

"W…what do you want from me. I don't make wishes, I've not seen any falling stars. I…I don't even buy lottery tickets." Rosa pushed her body into the corner of the couch, using her cat as a furry shield. He gave a shrill meow and leapt from her arms, trotting into the kitchen with his tail held high.

She was all alone with her little television friend. My God she was actually going over the edge.

"To answer your question, which I'm sure you are dying to know…"

"Could we please refrain from using such terms until we establish exactly *why* you are here?" Rosa croaked, staring warily at the woman.

"Oh heavens child, I'm no angel, they kicked me out of that union years ago. Nope, I am what you would call, for all intents and purposes, your Fairy Godmother."

"M…my Fairy Godmother?"

The woman cast her gaze to the ceiling. "Yes, it's a step down from angel's duty, granted, but the hours are so much better and the assignments are a heck of a lot more exciting."

"Did you say—Fairy Godmother?"

"And I thought it was old people who were hard of hearing. Listen up, I'll say it once more. Fae-ry God-mu-tha," she enunciated each syllable. Rosa noted then the thick Brooklyn accent.

She slipped from the couch and smiled at the strange image on the screen. Cautiously, she lowered the window leading to the fire escape. On top of everything else, she didn't need to have her neighbors hearing her talking to her TV. She paused at the window, her gaze drawn to the full moon above and the night sky shimmering with stars. Despite the city glare, she could see everything with crystal clarity. Had she never looked up?

"It's a beautiful world out there, you know."

Rosa turned and leaned against the windowsill, crossing

her arms over her chest. "Let's get something straight. I don't believe you're real." She tried to respond in the most emphatic manner she knew, certain that being rude would jar her out of whatever dream-like state she was in.

The old woman sighed.

"Why doesn't that surprise me? Very well, you leave me little choice."

In a cloud of purple haze, the woman re-appeared in full fairy regalia in the middle of Rosa's living room. A powdery lavender dust floated through the air, leaving a light film on her furniture and floor.

It was most certainly the least of her concerns.

"I can clean that up in a jiffy; we have much greater issues going on here."

As much as Rosa wished to refute that statement, she was careful not to even think of a wish, much less give this psycho woman a reason to use her hocus pocus on her. She glanced around, looking for a hidden projector. In the hands of a knowledgeable person, there was little that the right technology couldn't achieve. Maybe she was simply a holographic image being beamed in from a computer nearby. She checked behind her picture frame, under the couch cushions. Finally, she walked over, reached out and poked the woman's ample bosom.

Surprised, make that mortified, the old woman reared back in shock. Rosa responded in kind. The woman's gaze narrowed.

"Listen Princess, you have a few things to learn tonight and one of them is definitely trust."

"I don't trust anyone but myself."

"That much is clear." The old woman peered at her with kind eyes. Now dressed like a replica of Aunt Bea, from *Mayberry RFD*, she waved her hand and the purple residue disappeared.

Okay, *granted* Rosa couldn't explain that...not without some serious thought, anyway.

"The truth is my dear, you don't even truly trust yourself."

Rosa laughed. "That's ludicrous, I'm the most self-sufficient, reliable person I know."

"Which is why you sleep alone on your couch?" The old woman's head dipped as her twinkling blue eyes peered at her over her spectacles.

Much like Gerald, but not nearly as sexy.

Did she just think that?

"I choose to sleep on the couch," Rosa shrugged.

"Because?"

She hesitated a moment before answering, wondering if it was a trick question. "Because I choose to, that's why. There's no cosmic crime in sleeping on the couch is there?" It was Rosa's turn to laugh, but the woman looked at her with a somber gaze.

The elderly would-be fairy pulled a lace hanky from what appeared to be an oversized canvas bag. Two large knitting needles stuck out from the open top.

Rosa smiled. "Do you knit? I didn't think Fairy Godmothers had time for such menial human endeavors."

The silver–haired woman continued to clean her lenses.

"*That* attitude my dear, may well be part of your problem. You tend to see the glass half-empty, Rosa, instead of half-full."

Having had about enough, Rosa finely broke. "Okay, how much did *he* pay you to pull this little stunt?"

She adjusted the spectacles on her nose. "I have no idea what you're talking about, child."

"No? And just what are you knitting with those, pray tell, *Fairy Godmother?*" She knew she sounded snarky, but the woman was pushing her buttons and she had a campaign to design.

"These, you mean?" The woman plucked the needles, a ball of purple yarn, and a single thread from her bag.

"These are dreams, child. Each one is carefully tied and knotted as they are completed."

"That doesn't seem like you've been working on that one long." Rosa pointed out as she studied the short strand.

The old woman smiled. "That's why I'm here, Rosa. These represent everything in your life that you have wished for and received."

Rosa sank onto the couch, her gaze fixed on the very short strand of yarn. She began to realize how lonely and sequestered she'd become. A moment ticked by before she felt the cushions beside her give. The old woman took her hand, and patted it gently.

"It's never too late to have dreams, Rosa. But you have to be open to serendipity."

Rosa glanced at the old woman's hand holding hers. "I'm not built for, what did you call it, *serendipity?*"

Her Fairy Godmother patted her hand again.

"Of course you are. We just have to find it."

If this woman could help her, make her less afraid to believe in her dreams and find more than just work in her life, perhaps it would be wise to listen.

"You need to find the romance and the passion in your life, Rosa."

The old woman's kindly gaze held hers. True, Rosa couldn't attest that she had a smidgeon of romance in her, much less serendipity—whatever that was. The stakes always seemed too high to attain such luxuries. And besides, they weren't exactly reliable. She'd built her entire character on being reliable. "I don't know. Serendipity and romance? A person can get hurt and that can set you back from the practical goals in life."

"Does your practicality keep you warm on a cold night?" her Fairy Godmother asked, blue eyes sparkling wise with warm understanding.

"There's my cat, he sleeps at my feet." It was a particularly lame comeback, but all she had, sadly. Rosa shrugged. "Okay, you've made your point. However, in case you hadn't noticed, there aren't a million men breaking down my door to get in."

"Hum, I wonder why?" her Fairy Godmother commented as her gaze raked over Rosa's ragged sweatpants, her dirty pink fuzzy slippers, and spaghetti stained Dartmouth sweatshirt.

"Maybe I'm not interested in finding a Prince Charming," Rosa responded in her defense, though the truth was weakening her wobbly self-made fortress by the second.

"So, you do believe the idea that there might be one special someone out there, it's just that you're not interested?"

Rosa shrugged. "I don't know. I haven't found anyone yet that does anything for me." She pulled her legs up, wrapping her arms around her knees. Classic fetal position. She was in serious trouble. Rosa unlocked her arms, sitting up straight as she pressed her feet to the floor.

"What if I told you that you could find your Prince Charming and the ultimate ad campaign all at the same time?"

Rosa brightened, *that* was not a half-bad idea, in fact, it was brilliant. At least if the Prince part didn't work out she'd have the respect of the elderly board of directors for an effective ad campaign. "I'm listening."

"Are you willing to work with me?"

Rosa's gaze landed on the very short knitted chain representing her dreams. Struck with curiosity, she asked, "How far back do those go?"

"When was the last time you made a wish?"

Rosa bit her lip. She couldn't remember when she'd ever made a wish, probably as a child, but not in years. She glanced at the old woman. Really? What did she have to lose?

"Ok, what do I have to do?"

"It's simple really. You're in the mattress business. So we go with a time-tested recipe for such things. What you'll do is hold auditions for your next ad. You'll know your Prince Charming by how he is in bed."

Rosa's eyes widened. "Excuse me, I'm not *that* kind of girl."

"Yes, dear, we've established that," her Fairy Godmother laughed. "I'm kidding, sweetheart. You have such a delightful sense of humor. That's going to help." She pointed the end of her knitting needle at Rosa.

"So, you *aren't* asking me to sleep with them?" Rosa asked, mildly disappointed.

"Good heavens no, I use an ancient time-honored system. Very high success rate. I can give you references, of course."

"That won't be necessary," Rosa replied as she grabbed her sketchpad. "I can be open-minded if need be. Now tell me…how is this magical system going to help me?"

Rosa was getting comfortable with the idea of having her own Fairy Godmother. To be able to create a killer ad and have her deepest personal dreams come true. "Okay, I'm ready. Go slow; I want to catch every detail."

Her Fairy Godmother folded her lace hanky and stuffed it under her bra strap.

"It starts with a pea."

Rosa wrote the letter on the sketchpad and waited, her pencil poised for the rest.

"That's it," the old woman replied, tucking the yarn and needles back into her bag.

"But, wait a minute, what does 'P' mean?"

The kind woman shifted her starry blue gaze to Rosa's and smiled.

"You'll see."

❧

Two days later Gerald arrived for work and had to push through the crowded mass of humanity huddled around the display window of *Sweet Slumber*. Outside, camera crews from television stations and a photography studio blocked the building's entrance.

A burly man in a blue jumpsuit, carrying a coil of electrical cable over his arm and a coffee cup in his hand smashed into Gerald, splashing coffee down the front of his freshly pressed white dress shirt. As he tried to pull the scalding heat from his torso, a cab whizzed by sending an arc of rainwater over his just dry-cleaned suit pants, splattering them with mud.

A delivery boy trying to make his way through the crowd, skidded inches from Gerald who had to jump out of his way and in so doing fell backwards into a cement planter filled with flowers that had recently been watered. He felt the dampness soak clear through his trousers and into his boxer briefs. He was about to call it quits and head back home when he heard pounding on the window behind him. There was Rosa, his beautiful dream girl, staring at him with a wild look of fear or confusion etched on her lovely face. Soaked boxers be damned, he had a duty to see to his lovely damsel in distress. He pushed from the planter, hiding his muddy tush as best he could with his briefcase as he pushed through the front doors of the building. It took him a few moments to wind through the bevy of electrical cords and reporters stationed outside the large room where they staged displays for the window. Once there, however, he ran into another obstacle, more unusual than anything he'd seen thus far. The entrance to the room was blocked by an elderly woman, legs locked, her gaze steely, and arms crossed over her ample chest. She reminded him a lot of his Aunt Agatha, whom everyone referred to affectionately as 'Attila.'

His disheveled appearance, he knew, wasn't much help as he stepped ahead of the crowd.

"Excuse me, I need to get inside." Gerald pushed a shock of hair from his eyes. Damn, his gel wasn't working today, either. Great.

"Yeah, that's what they all say," the old woman replied, her eyes raking over his muddy, wet-with-coffee and *Miracle Grow*-mulched apparel.

"You don't understand, Miss. This is about Rosa, she needs me."

One silvery brow arched as she peered over her glasses. "So you say. Very well, and how long have you known Ms. O'Flannery?" Her blue eyes studied him.

Was this a game? Gerald was getting frustrated. This old broad was about as nosy as Attila—his Aunt Agatha—too.

"Listen, Rosa and I have worked together a very long time. She just knocked on the window and I could see by the look on her face that she was in trouble. Now if you don't let me in there, I'm, well…I may have to get physical." Gerald pulled back his shoulders, straightening to his full six foot-two frame.

The old woman smiled and her blue eyes twinkled. Not in a grandmotherly way, but weird, like a WarCraft wizard.

"Physical? That's what I'm hoping," she muttered, and opened the door, standing aside to let him through.

There was a rush of young men behind him bolting forward to the door. Gerald heard the old woman from behind as the door closed.

"Sorry guys, private shoot going on. Don't make me get

out the flying monkeys, now move on back."

Gerald searched through the sheets of plastic photographer's drapery hanging from the ceiling and finally found Rosa, perusing names on a clipboard. She looked up, her expression filled with pure panic.

"I haven't found the right one yet."

"Excuse me?" He pushed his glasses up the bridge of his nose.

"I haven't found my Royal Prince."

He thought for a moment and realized it was for her ad. "Oh, you mean, for your presentation?"

She held his gaze. "Of course, that's what I mean. What on earth happened to you?" She took him in from head to toe.

"Um, it's a long story. You see, I was walking down the sidewalk when…"

"Gerald, I haven't got time, its nine-fifteen and I have to make my presentation to the board in forty-five minutes and none of these men are good in bed."

She waved her clipboard under his nose.

It was his turn to be surprised. "My, you work fast." He grinned, though his stomach had a funny feeling, like knitted shoelaces or when his socks get all tangled up in his dryer.

She slanted him a side-glance. "Funny. But the truth is, none of these guys meet the standards of the…" Rosa stopped short, chewing on the corner of her lip as she often did when she was thinking. He had the sudden urge to make her stop thinking all together. *Not a good time, Gerald.*

"Of the…?" He waited for her to finish her thought, but was willing for her to take all the time she needed. He could stand here all day just to smell the scent of her soft perfumed skin.

She groaned and dropped the clipboard to the floor. He stopped to pick it up and she took it from him without so much as a thanks.

"Uh," Gerald blinked, "is there anything I can do to help?"

"Yeah, well, you don't happen to know any good-looking guys, do you?"

Ouch. "Uh, well, what about me?" It was a bold move, even

for him. He felt as naked as a Thanksgiving turkey.

"What about you?" She rubbed her temple. "Oh, sure, no problem. Of course, I'll give you credit for whomever you can find. Time is of the essence and it's better that we present this ad together than neither one of us having a plan."

"What makes you think I don't have my plan ready?" he answered, frustrated that she didn't get that he'd offered himself for her ad.

"Gerald, please, I don't have time for this. Are you going to help me or not?"

He put his ego aside. "Give me five minutes. What does the guy have to do?"

"Great. Thanks. Gerald, I owe you one. I have to go check on those reporters outside, but if you could get the guy down to his skivvies and get him in bed, on his side, propped on his elbow. I want that sexy, passionate 'I'm-waiting-for-you-only' look in his eyes. The photographer will do the rest."

She slapped the clipboard to his chest. "You think you can handle that?"

He gazed down at her warm, dark eyes the color of his *Starbuck's* espresso. "Yeah, I think I can."

"Great. I don't know who you have in mind, but right now, Gerald, you are my knight in shining armor." With that, she pushed up on her toes and kissed his cheek.

The next moment, she was gone. The story of his life.

Rosa pushed aside the draperies and squeezed through the door to the lobby. With her back plastered against the door, she beheld the throng of reporters, curious on-lookers, and well-dressed models all clamoring for attention. And in their midst stood her Fairy Godmother, expertly staving them from battering down the door.

Rosa inched to her side and whispered as her gaze roved over the crowd. "How are we doing, FG?"

"Piece of cake. I haven't had this much fun since the dwarves got rowdy at the royal wedding and they had to call us in for crowd control. Gingerbread men can get pretty crazy. My guess, it's all those spices."

"I think we may have this handled. Gerald said he'd find me the right guy."

"And you trust this Gerald?" Her Fairy Godmother eyed her warily.

Rosa tossed back a frown. "Well, yeah, he's a geek, but he's trustworthy and he works very hard. No, he won't let me down." Rosa paused a moment as she thought of her response. "I haven't always been very nice to him and that makes me feel bad. Maybe when all this is over I can do something to make it up to him." She shrugged.

Her Fairy Godmother smiled brightly. "Yeah, well, maybe. I'll take care of this crowd and you take care of the reporters. What's our time?"

Rosa glanced at her watch. "Nine-twenty five."

"Let's do this," her Fairy Godmother stated, crossing her arms over her chest.

⁓

With the reporters appeased, the models dismissed, and the crowd beginning to disperse, Rosa took a deep breath, pleased that her Fairy Godmother had magically seen to the breaking up of the crowd in less than two minutes, thirty-six seconds. Rosa scurried inside the room, closing her eyes and the door simultaneously, drinking in the serene quiet of the photo shoot area. She heard the muffled sound of a man's voice giving instructions and, curious, began to follow it. There was a lot less chaos going on, less people falling over one another, and she offered up silent thanks to Gerald for getting things under control so efficiently. Maybe she'd take him up on that lunch he was forever trying to ask her for if, in fact, he ever asked her again. Perhaps she would first need to take the plunge and apologize for her standoffish behavior.

Rosa stepped around a drapery and her heart came to a sudden standstill.

"Can we drape that just over his hip? We want to entice, not shoot a porn movie here, people." The photographer snapped off another few pictures, oblivious to her presence. Rosa stepped from the shadows, her eyes glued on the gorgeous man propped up in the 'Royal Slumber' bed, his muscular torso and washboard abs contrasted against the white cotton sheets.

"Gerald?" It came out in a whisper. Damn, Gerald cleaned up good, *real*good.

His gaze found Rosa's from across the room and he gave her a smile that made the back of her knees weak. It spoke to her of passionate nights, a pair of strong arms around her to keep her safe and warm, a friend who didn't require liver snaps to come home to every night.

"That's it! That's the look, hang on to that, Gerry, that's perfect. Ok, kids, that's a wrap. We've got our ad." The photographer passed by Rosa with a wide grin on his face. "Not sure where you were hiding him, darling, but he's dynamite. Don't let that one out of your sight. I'll leave the memory card on your desk, just plug it into your laptop." He glanced back at Gerald and made a low growl in his throat, the crew following dutifully behind as he left the set.

Rosa couldn't stop staring at the gorgeous looking man in bed, imagining him in hers.

"Gerald?"

He grinned, showing that adorable and plum sexy dimple. "Is this *'I'm-waiting-for-you-only' enough?*"

Rosa went weak in the knees and swallowed. Oh yeah, it was. Unfortunately, it appeared he'd failed the magical prince part of the test. Maybe her Fairy Godmother was wrong. Her heart squeezed tightly.

"You're perfect, absolutely perfect," she sighed wistfully.

"Well." He grinned as he rubbed his hand over the sheet beside him. "That's something you may have to research for yourself."

Rosa sucked in her breath at his bold statement. She already had a delightful image of the two of them, but she didn't know how to tell him about her Godmother's 'magical system.' What if Gerald was good only for her ad, but not as her Prince Charming?

"Um, are you quite comfortable then...on that mattress?" She took a few steps, stopping short of the end of the bed.

He shifted his long legs beneath the sheet and the mere

whisper-soft rustle caused Rosa's blood to heat. She bit back a moan.

"As much as a guy can be stripped down to next to nothing in a room full of people...and you?" he asked with a lop-sided grin.

Rosa shivered. "Yeah," she offered a weak laugh. Despite how incredible he looked, how much she was utterly drawn to him, he hadn't passed the test of the 'pea.' Her Fairy Godmother stated clearly that *her* Prince would be susceptible to even the slightest discomfort beneath the mattress.

A lump formed in Rosa's throat as she prepared to let him down easy. "Listen, there's something I have to tell you, Gerald."

"Okay, but come here, I have something to tell you first." He crooked his finger, motioning her to come closer, checking over her shoulder as though making sure they were alone.

Rosa stood stiff at the side of the bed, her hands fisted, telling herself to be strong.

"Come closer, so I can whisper this, I don't want anyone else to hear; and honestly, I'd appreciate it if what I'm about to say stays between us, okay?"

Rosa leaned down. His face was inches from hers, his aftershave and the scent of rainwater fogged her brain. She nodded. What a shame to find out that after all of this that Gerald really wasn't her perfect match. Maybe her Fairy Godmother was having an off day. She studied his face without his glasses. His sturdy jaw, the little laugh lines at the corner of those beautiful hazel eyes.

"You have the most fantastic eyes for a woman." Gerald tucked a tendril of hair over her ear.

She held her hands up, clasping them together in front of her, realizing how much she wanted to touch him. "Gerald, just what was it that you wished to tell me?" Rosa's eyes drifted to his mouth and she forced her gaze back to his.

"So, here's the deal. Frankly, have you ever laid on one of these mattresses? They are the most ungodly awful things on the face of the planet. I've never felt such a lumpy mattress in all my life."

Rosa's legs gave out and she lowered herself to the edge of the bed, her eyes glued to his. "Really? You wanted to tell me that this mattress is lumpy, that you are totally uncomfortable lying here?"

He shifted to face her. "I know, it's crazy, right? All these years and I never once laid down on one of these things. Have you?"

Rosa threw herself at him, slamming his back to the bed. "Oh my Godmother. You're my Prince."

With a sexy grin he turned her beneath him and stared down at her. His hazel eyes burned with passion.

"I'll be anything you need," he whispered just before he kissed her.

In the shadows, Rosa's Fairy Godmother grinned as she held up the shiny green pea and dropped it into her bag. She pulled out her knitting and happily secured the first of many dreams come true for Rosa.

And as for Gerald and Rosa? They lived happily, of course, rarely sleeping on their Royal Slumber mattress.

The End

Award-winning author, Amanda McIntyre loves to write stories featuring unique characters, twisted plots, and plenty of romance.

You can visit her on the web at www.amandamcintyre.net.

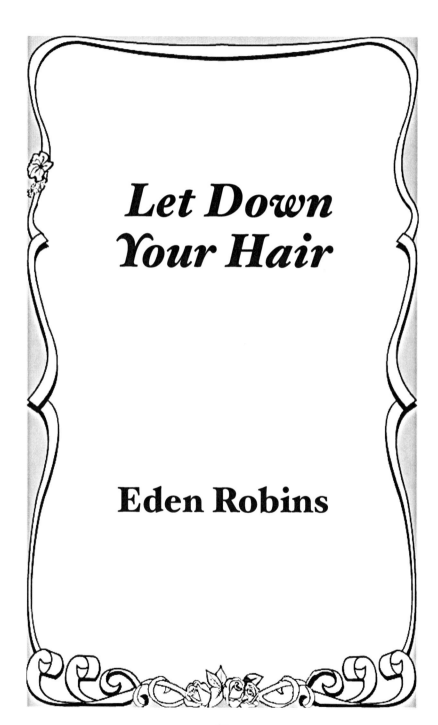

Let Down Your Hair

Eden Robins

Rapunzel, Rapunzel, let down your hair.

The children surrounding her chanted mockingly. They laughed and pointed to where she lay sprawled out on the pavement. She had been pushed down by Suzanne Thompson. Suzanne was twelve years old, stood taller than any other girl or boy in the school, had a loud, bellowing voice you could hear down the hall, and was tough as nails. You didn't mess with Suzie or you got hurt. Even at the age of ten, she knew that. All you could do was hope the older girl did whatever she was going to do to you, and got it over with quickly.

Suzie had chosen the last day of school, right before summer break, to pick on her.

Again.

It wasn't the first time. With a name like Rapunzel, it didn't take much for the other kids to tease her. And with Suzie as their leader, they eagerly joined in.

"Why'd your mom give you such a stupid name, anyway?" Suzie asked, shoving her down again as she tried to stand up. She fell back to the ground, almost hitting her head from the force of the older girl's push. "Is it because you're stupid? Or maybe it's because you have long blond hair, just like Rapunzel? No, I know what it is. It's because your parents think you're so ugly and weird that you should be locked away in a tower somewhere. Yeah, I bet that's it. It's weird the way you read books all the time, and don't talk to other kids. You're nothing but an ugly weirdo."

Ugly weirdo, ugly weirdo, ugly weirdo.

All the kids chanted it over and over again. Rapunzel felt tears start to form in her eyes, but held them back, barely. She was scared, and her feelings were hurt, but more than that she was mad. Mad at her mom for giving her such a dumb name, and mad at Suzie and the other kids for picking on her.

"What's the matter, ugly weirdo? Gonna cry like a baby?"

Something snapped in Rapunzel then and there. She'd had enough. Shooting to her feet before anyone could stop her, she pulled back her hand, made a fist, and hit Suzie Thompson in the nose as hard as she could.

The crowd instantly grew silent.

"You broke my nose! You broke my nose!" Suzie cried out as she covered it with her hands. Tears flowed from the older girl's eyes, which were now filled with fear.

"You stay away from me! You hear me, Rapunzel? You stay away!" Suzie screamed, backing away, then turning and running away until she was out of sight.

Rapunzel looked around her at the other kids. Most of their mouths hung open, and their eyes were filled with shock. She was shocked, too. She couldn't believe she had just done that. But now that she had, she wanted to finish what she started. She was tired of being picked on.

She raised her fist, and slowly spun around, shaking it at the other kids.

"Anybody else want to tease me about my name?"

No one said a thing.

Rapunzel lowered her fist.

"Good. Then just leave me alone. And you tell Suzie that the next time she sees me, she better leave me alone, too, or I'll hit her again."

And with that last threat, Rapunzel pushed through the circle of kids surrounding her, and stormed away.

❧

Twenty-eight years later…

"What do you mean she's sick?" Rapunzel asked.

"She's sick, Pun, what more do you need to know?" her little brother asked, using her childhood nickname. When he was little, Tim couldn't say Rapunzel, no matter how hard he tried. Her parents tried to help him by pronouncing it slowly over and over again, but his little toddler mouth couldn't form the word. Five years his senior, she took pity on him, and told him to just call her 'Pun'. From that moment on, the name stuck. Tim called her that to this day.

"You need to fly back here ASAP. She's been asking for you."

"Tim, are you sure? You know how dramatic Mom gets. And she's been asking me to come home for years. Especially after Dan and I got divorced."

"This is different, Pun. The doctors are really concerned, and so am I," her brother explained, the worry evident in his voice. It wasn't like her brother to get so anxious. If he was that worried about their mother, then there was a very good reason. "Just come home, Sis, okay?"

"Okay, Tim," she said with a sigh. It was going to be hell getting away from work, but if her mother were truly that sick, she wanted to be there for her, despite their differences. "I'll tie up a few loose ends here, and fly home as soon as possible. Most likely some time tomorrow."

"Thanks. I really think she means it this time, and I know Mom would appreciate having you here," Tim said in a relieved voice.

After hanging up, Rapunzel quickly showered and dressed. As usual, her attire meant little more than functionality to her. Since high school she had worn her hair short, trying to keep the rebellious, curly blond locks in control. The style was simple and easy to care for.

That same summer she had hit Suzanne Thompson, Rapunzel had a growth spurt. She went back to school that fall almost as tall as the older girl. Suzie never bothered her again. Although she was glad about that, her new size had some disadvantages. The remaining two years of grade school the other kids whispered about her behind her back. Still, she managed to hear every insult. They called her names like "Amazon woman" or "Blond Giant," or even just "Big Blond Freak".

After graduating from eighth grade, Rapunzel decided that

it was time to cut her long blond hair. Her mother hadn't known what she was going to do. In fact her mom had always insisted Rapunzel keep her locks long so that she looked more "girlish". But once she had decided to do it, and came home with the deed done, her mother could do little about it, besides complain, which she did in spades.

"How could you do that without talking to me first? You know how much I love your long hair, dear."

Rapunzel had stuck to her guns.

"Well, I don't, mom. I'm ready for a change, and I think I'm old enough to decide how I keep my hair."

Her mom's eyes widened.

"But you're only, you're only…"

"I'm thirteen, Mom," she interrupted, puffing out her chest and raising her chin defiantly. "A teenager. All the other girls' moms let them choose how they want their hair. Why can't you be more like them?"

Rapunzel had wanted to take the words back the minute she said them.

Her mother's reaction was immediate.

Tears filling her eyes, she held her hand to her chest dramatically.

"That wasn't nice, Rapunzel. You know I'm sick. And you know I'm doing the best I can. I can't handle this right now. I need to lay down, but rest assured your father will hear about this when he gets home. And he'll handle you. Until then you stay in your room, young lady. I'm going to bed."

Her father grounded her for a week for not asking first, but then smiled and whispered to her that he liked her new hair style. Her mom eventually accepted Rapunzel's decision to cut her hair, but still complained about it, even after her daughter grew to adulthood. Rapunzel never looked back after that first cut. Cutting her hair had been the best choice for breaking out of her "Big Blond Freak" label. Going into high school, all she had wanted was to fit in, to be like other girls, a good friend and a girl who boys would like.

That attitude carried over into adulthood. She kept her appearance professional and low key, yet she didn't try to hide the fact that she was a woman. The cut of her suits were always feminine and her make up lightly and carefully applied. She didn't want to hide the fact that she was a woman, but she also didn't want her gender to be an obstacle to her career in a field that was very testosterone driven. Her training at the police academy taught her that lesson. And in her current career as a personal security specialist, it was imperative that she be judged objectively based only on her disciplined work performance.

Due to the one-on-one nature of her work, Rapunzel didn't have much leeway for last minute vacations or getaways. Despite this, she managed to put together a list of things to do to ease her spur of the moment departure. As luck would have it, she was in between cases. Although scheduled to meet with a new client that week, she was able to give her case to another specialist to handle.

She managed to get a flight home to Boston the next day, for a ridiculous price. Luckily, as part owner of Solid Security, her income kept her quite comfortable. She and her partner, Louis Redfield, managed a good living between the cases they each took on, and the ones they gave to their employed specialists. She and Louis had met at the police academy, become friends, and had stayed in contact after graduation. After working several years on the streets, they both came to the conclusion that personal security was the way to go. More money, better hours, and being their own bosses appealed to both of them. And since neither of them had married since starting on the force, they each had put away enough of a nest egg to embark on their joint venture.

Driving from the airport, Rapunzel studied her surroundings. The October weather in New England still took her breath away. Sick of the cold weather back East, she had gone to college in Arizona, and after graduating from ASU decided to stay. Her small home in the historic Encanto district of Phoenix was in a green belt area with large lush trees and green grass front lawns instead of the typical rock desert landscape so many Arizona residents preferred. Yet it still couldn't hold a candle to the foliage of the North East The autumn colors of orange, red, brown, yellow and green were so vivid and varied it almost hurt her eyes to look at them.

As Rapunzel drove her rental car through the tree-lined streets that marked the historic neighborhood in Salem where her parents lived, she couldn't stop her mind from drifting back to a time long ago, when she was driving along these same streets away from home, away from everything she knew to head out to the "wild west" of Arizona.

Her mother had been sick, again, and her father had to work that day, so they had asked their neighbors, the Seevers, if they would drive her to the airport. It turned out they were busy as well, but their son, Jack, volunteered.

"I'll be glad to take you to the airport," he had offered, standing in the doorway of her parent's house the night before she was scheduled to leave.

"No, that's really not necessary. I'm sure I can get one of my friends to take me," Rapunzel had said, struggling to maintain her composure.

"Nonsense, Rapunzel," her father said frowning at her. "Of course we'll accept your offer, Jack. I'd feel much better knowing it was you who were driving her into Boston."

Strolling up to the doorway where they stood, her father smiled at Jack. "I really appreciate the offer, too. I'd take my daughter, but I have an important meeting tomorrow, and Agatha is still not feeling well."

Rapunzel had tried to maintain calm despite the out of control panic that was sending her heart speeding out of control.

"No, Dad. I'm sure Jack has a lot going on also. He's got to get ready to go back to school as well."

Jack lifted an eyebrow and smiled mockingly at her.

"No problem, Mr. Adams. I'll be glad to take your daughter to the airport."

Although he was talking to her father, Jack was staring straight at her, and the light of amusement in his eyes was impossible to miss. Rapunzel couldn't help but squirm under his stare. Jack had always had that power over her. He could just look at her a certain way, and she started getting squirmy.

"It's settled then. Thanks again, Jack. We'll see you bright and early tomorrow morning," her dad said as he slowly closed the door.

The last thing she saw before the front door shut was Jack's arrogant smile and a quick wink. Rapunzel had swung around, furious and frustrated. She tried to remain calm, but the thought of driving into town with Jack was already frazzling her nerves.

It wasn't that she hadn't liked Jack back then. They had been neighbors since they were little kids, and had spent a lot of time together when they were younger. Although they played hide and seek, tag, as well as various sports together, more often than not imaginary games were what they played most. And somehow she had always ended up pretending to be the princess in jeopardy, and he the prince coming to save her. The funny thing was, no matter how much Rapunzel had balked at this, no matter how much she had explained to Jack that she could save herself, he had always insisted on being her knight in shining armor.

"I'll save you, don't worry," he would say with a very serious look on his face.

"You're not the boss of me, Jack. I can save myself," she had said one time in particular, puffing her eight-year-old chest out proudly. "I don't need you to do it for me."

"C'mon, let me save you. I have a really great plan," he had cajoled, smiling widely with a mischievous look in his eyes that had always left her just curious enough to agree.

And without exception, he managed to not only to save her, but to leave both of them laughing with delight at the end of the game, mainly because he chose very unorthodox ways of saving her, probably to bypass her objections. Like instead of killing the dragon that was holding her captive, he would persuade her to bake a pretend giant dragon cake, then feed it to the dragon until he blew up from eating too much.

They had spent many a lazy summer days and cool fall afternoons pretending to be different people, in different worlds, on fantastical adventures. They had been as thick as thieves, until puberty hit. Jack was a couple of years older than her, so when he turned thirteen, things had changed. He had changed. And they had just stopped being friends.

Despite that, Rapunzel had been very aware of Jack when she started high school. He had been a junior and she a freshman, yet he still made the time to come over and talk to her whenever he saw her on campus. He was the All-American type, playing various sports and participating in student government as junior vice president, then senior president of his class. Jack was even voted most popular his senior year at their high school. But he had never been snobby or mean to her, and he had never once teased her about her hair or her size like the other kids had. She suspected almost every girl at the school had been a little in love with Jack Seevers.

Rapunzel had been no exception.

The ride to the airport that next day had been uncomfortable, to say the least.

"So, you're running away again, little girl?" Jack had asked right after they had begun their drive into Boston.

Rapunzel bristled. They hadn't talked, really talked, since before high school, and now, just because of what had happened between them over the summer he was getting personal?

"I'm no little girl, Jack," she had said glaring at him. "And I don't run away. I fight my own battles."

"Yes, you do," he had agreed with a nod, and a wistful smile that told her he was remembering exactly how often she insisted on doing just that. "You do as long as you can be in control of those battles. But the minute things get a little out of control, the minute you lose a handle on things or get out of your box, you put the brakes on and high tail it back to your safe ivory tower. You and I both know that first hand too, Pun."

"I told you not to…"

Rapunzel bit her tongue until tears formed in her eyes.

She had started to tell him not to call her that nickname, to tell him that it was reserved only for her brother, but she knew by then it was no use. Ever since he had heard Tim call her that as children, he did the same. The endearment had been hard to swallow coming from him at a time when they were about to

46

be separated for who knows how long.

If it had only been that they were childhood friends that grew apart, maybe it would have been less emotional. But that summer after her high school graduation, before she left Salem for college, things had changed. Jack and she had bumped into each other at a summer party, and something sparked to life between them. It had been an enlightening evening for both of them. They had rediscovered one another somehow. And it had been incredible. They had spent the mild summer days getting to know each other better, learning about each other now that they were older, and having fun.

And their friendship had developed into something more intimate and mature.

But in the end that hadn't mattered. What had mattered to Rapunzel by the end of that summer was that Jack was dangerous. Dangerous to her state of mind, dangerous to everything she knew and held tightly to. Jack had wanted her to take a leap she just hadn't been prepared to make, so she backed off. Things hadn't worked out. And she had known they never would.

Instead, she decided to look ahead and move forward without him.

And Jack had let her go.

The words of Josh Turner's song, "Go With Me," playing on the car radio suddenly registered.

"Would you go with me, if we rode the clouds together?"

She returned to the present as she passed Jack's parents' house and pulled into the driveway of her old home. That was the same question Jack had asked her way back when. He had asked her to fly with him. He had asked her to forget about everything but the two of them, forget about her worries and insecurities, and forget about her need to get away from her mother's overwhelming presence in her life. Jack had asked her to trust what they had.

Then he had asked her to marry him.

And she had said no.

Turning the engine off, Rapunzel shrugged her purse over her shoulder and stepped out of her car. All things came to an end. They had just been kids. What had they known? What had he known?

"Daydreaming again, Pun?"

Rapunzel was jerked out of her reverie as the object of her thoughts and memories stood in front of her. And what a sight he was. Shirt off, loose jeans lying low on his hips and a smile that still knocked her off balance. She could only guess at what Jack got away with when he smiled like that at a woman. She imagined just about anything. Knowing first hand what that grin did to her, she tried to steel herself against its power.

"Still running around wild and half naked, Jack?"

Jack stepped closer, his eyes narrowed lazily and his smile widened to wolfish proportions.

"I never heard you complain about that the last summer we were together," he said in a low, sexy voice that made her stomach tighten in anticipation.

Rapunzel took a step back. She needed to put some space between them.

Raising her chin proudly, she did her best to look cool and unaffected.

"That was then, and this is now. I'm over it. Aren't you?"

Jack stepped closer, so close she could feel his body heat, and smell his spicy, sweaty, all male scent. Instead of putting her off, it immediately sent her libido skyrocketing. Jack had always had a knack for doing that.

"So, you're completely over it, are you?"

Rapunzel tried to put some space between them once more, but instead of separating them as she had hoped; she merely bumped the side of her car as she backed into it. Panic filled her as the impact of Jack's proximity made her knees weak. She had nowhere to run.

"No running away this time, is there Pun?" Jack asked, as if he had been reading her mind.

Placing a hand against the car on either side of her head, he had her neatly boxed in.

Rapunzel managed to maintain her composure and meet Jack's stare.

"I don't need to run, and I don't need to be saved any

longer, Jack. I can take care of myself."

And with those words, Rapunzel ducked under Jack's arms and strode toward her front door.

"Nice seeing you again, Jack. Take care," she called over her shoulder.

Before she could ring the front doorbell, Jack caught up with her.

"Wait. Maybe I didn't handle that reunion so well. Let's start again."

Rapunzel turned to him.

His charming smile was hard to resist.

"Why?"

"Because I'd like to catch up on your life, hear how you've been doing. I've thought a lot about you over the years."

"Really?" she asked, finding it hard to believe that Jack found the time in his busy life as a judge to think about a childhood friend.

He nodded his head.

"Definitely," he assured her. "I took the week off to spend time with my folks and help them with things around the house. They aren't getting any younger and I know it's a lot harder for them to maintain their place. Mowing their lawn was the last thing on my "To Do" list. How about having a drink with me while you're in town?"

"I'll only be here for a couple of nights, and my mom's not feeling well."

"Make the time. Please?" he interrupted softly.

The sincerity in his eyes was her undoing.

"Okay. How about tomorrow night?" she asked with a shy smile. Suddenly she felt like she was back in high school, with the popular boy asking her out. "I need to spend some time with my family, make sure Mom's going to be okay first, and then I can go from there. Can I call you tomorrow morning and let you know what's happening?"

Jack smiled then.

Her heart did somersaults.

He had the nicest smile.

"Sure. Here's my number."

Rapunzel punched Jack's mobile number into her phone before ringing the front door. With a last wave, she watched him go back to his parent's yard and continue mowing the lawn. While she waited for someone to answer the door, she couldn't help admiring how good the man looked. Since neither of them were youngsters, and he older than she, he obviously worked hard at staying in shape.

As he disappeared from sight, the thought of seeing him again seemed very appealing.

"You made it!"

Rapunzel's thoughts changed like the wind as she turned in time to see her brother, Tim, close in on her and give her a big bear hug.

"It's, um, nice to see you too little brother, but if you don't stop squeezing me, uh, so tightly I'm going to pass out. I can't breathe!"

"Sorry, sis," Tim said with a chuckle, as he released her. "I'm just so glad to see you. And your timing worked out perfectly. I mentioned to Mom yesterday that you would be coming home, and she perked right up. She's looking forward to seeing you."

Rapunzel wasn't so sure about that, but she just smiled and walked into the house with her brother.

⁂

"You look really great," Jack said the next night. They were sitting in a little pub in Old Salem that had been there forever. The Corky Pig was well known; the beer was usually dark, thick, frothy, and icy cold, and the clientele lively and fun.

It was Friday night, so the place was really hopping. Somehow, Jack managed to find the two of them a quiet corner table where they could talk.

"Thanks," she said with a little smile. "You're not so bad yourself."

Jack's grin grew sexy and self-assured.

From that point forward the two of them just seemed to "click" back into place. They discussed her mother's health. That morning, after seeing how weak and run down her mother had been the night before, she had called her mom's doctor to find out exactly what was going on. The doctor told her that it was yet another flare up, but that she had leveled off. As usual, the doctor hadn't mentioned her mother's alcoholism, or the severe affect it was having on her health, other than to remark that she was deteriorating quickly.

Her mother had been an alcoholic for as long as Rapunzel could remember. Her continual bouts of illness, where she wouldn't get out of bed for days, were really drinking binges. Her father and brother were in denial about it, but Rapunzel and her mother had come to blows over it several times since she was a teenager and discovered the truth.

Luckily she and her mother's visit last night had been peaceful. Other than asking her to get back with her ex-husband and move home to Salem, which she always did when her daughter was home, her mother and she had gotten along fairly well. But her mom didn't look good. Rapunzel was worried because she looked frail, weak, shaky, and depressed. The depression was nothing new to her mother, but now she was also despondent, not seeming to care much about anything. That worried her.

That last summer together, before she went off to college in Arizona, she and Jack talked about her mother's problem. Jack had told her that he and many of their neighbors and friends knew exactly what her mother's illness was. Her alcoholism was no secret, yet no one discussed it openly.

Except she and Jack. And now was no different. As they sat in the pub together, it was as if they had never lost touch with each other.

"Has her drinking gotten worse?" he asked.

"No. I don't think so. But she's slowly, but surely, killing herself. Her health has deteriorated dramatically since I saw her three months ago. And I feel so helpless, because nothing I say or do has ever deterred her from that course."

"You know you can't control what choices your mother makes, Pun. It's up to her, just as it's always been up to her."

"I know, Jack. But it's so difficult to sit back and watch my mother continue to destroy her life."

They talked through dinner and drinks, catching up as the

live band played its 'oldies but goodies' set. Several hours later, the pub's owners told them it was time to go home. They both looked around the place surprised to see that there were no customers left in the place.

"I guess we lost track of time," Jack said. "We better get going."

Rapunzel nodded her head.

"We wouldn't want to be thrown out," Rapunzel said with a teasing smile.

Jack shook his head and grinned as he laid his hand at the small of her back and led her outside to his car.

"Nope, we wouldn't want that. Not after such a fantastic reunion."

The ride home was quick, and before they realized it, they were standing on her parents' front porch saying goodnight.

"I had a really nice time, Jack. I'm sorry about your divorce, but it sounds like you've spent the last two years since then creating a great life for yourself."

"Thanks, Pun. I feel pretty good about that, too. And you should also. It sounds like you've done a lot with your life since your divorce. I can't say I'm sorry it happened though. Because if it hadn't, you wouldn't be standing here tonight waiting for me to kiss you."

Rapunzel raised an eyebrow at that.

"What makes you think I'm waiting for you to kiss me?"

Jack grinned. It was all male.

"I can just tell."

Rapunzel's eyes narrowed as she studied Jack.

"Really?"

He nodded his head.

"Yep. And I really would love to oblige you, Pun. But I don't kiss on the first date. It's policy of mine. So, no matter how much you want it, there will be no kissing tonight."

Rapunzel couldn't believe her ears. Of all the arrogant, fat-headed men! How dare he assume that he was so irresistible to women?

But you do want him to kiss you, don't you?

Rapunzel shook her head as she imagined his warm lips

touching hers.

No!

It didn't matter what she did or didn't want. How dare he try to dictate her behavior? That was sexist and egotistical, and, well, she would just show him.

Stepping forward, Rapunzel curled her fingers around each side of his shirt collar, pulled him close, and kissed Jack with all she was worth. Some time later she realized he had his arms around her, and was now the one dominating the situation. Her back against the wall, his body pressed close to hers, and he making love to her mouth in a way that drove her nuts. Gentle, yet firm, teasing yet demanding. It was all she could do to stay upright. Her legs felt like wet noodles, and she couldn't seem to catch her breath.

When he finally started to pull away, she realized her hands were still firmly clutched around his collar. She felt a blush creep up her cheeks. After a minute, the fog cleared and she managed to unclench her fingers so Jack could lean away from her.

"Boy," he said with a low whistle. "You sure showed me."

Rapunzel's gaze swung to his face and her eyes narrowed suspiciously. Jack fought not to smile, but the corners of his mouth kept curling upward despite his efforts. Finally, he let his smile go and a small chuckle escaped.

"Oh! That was a dirty trick," she said, giving him a light slap on the shoulder.

"What do you mean?" he asked, eyes wide, attempting to look innocent. "All I told you was my policy. You took it from there, Pun."

Rapunzel rolled her eyes and turned to unlock the front door.

"Whatever," she said.

"Are you running away again?"

Rapunzel swung around, eyes flaring.

"What do you mean?"

Jack folded his arms over his chest and looked down at her arrogantly.

"You know exactly what I mean. When are you going to

quit running away to your ivory tower? When are you going to let yourself feel and live, Pun?"

Placing her hands on her hips, she glared at him.

"I live my life, Jack. I am living life just the way I want to."

"That's not living, Pun. That's going through the motions. That's controlling every situation, every event, every place and person in your life so you feel safe. Don't you think it's time to stop keeping such a tight rein on everything?"

"I don't know what you're talking about, Jack. But I do know that this sounds very familiar to the last conversation you and I had together before I went off to college."

"That's because it is the same conversation. You're still living in your glass bubble, afraid to break out, afraid to truly be who you are. You're afraid to let down your hair."

"Very funny. Nice play on words, Jack. Would you like to quote the whole text of *Rapunzel* now?" she asked sarcastically.

Jack let out an exasperated breath and ran his fingers through his hair impatiently.

"If it will help you let go and live your own life, then I'll do whatever the hell you want, Pun. I know we've been apart for a long time, but I know what I see, feel, and want. I see you protecting yourself by trying to be in control of everything, hoping that will keep you safe and save you from being like your mother. I feel the same thing I felt for you when we were just kids. A connection I've never felt with anyone else. And I want you in a way I haven't wanted a woman for a very long time."

Rapunzel's mouth hung open in shock. She didn't know how to respond.

"That's all I have to say. Goodnight, Pun. I enjoyed spending the evening with you. I know you're leaving tomorrow. But if you ever decide to break out of your ivory tower and let down that beautiful hair of yours," he offered, giving her a quick peck on the cheek before turning to leave, "I'll be around. Give me a call."

Rapunzel was speechless. She must have looked ridiculous, standing there, mouth hanging open, silently watching him walk away.

After a minute her thoughts cleared and she went inside. She headed straight for the kitchen. Everyone was sleeping, and the house was almost completely dark, except for the stove light her mother always left on. She had done that for as long as Rapunzel could remember. That light had always represented a beacon of safety and hope for her. She wasn't sure why. Maybe because it had been one of the few stable things her mother had done. Regardless of how she felt, or what was going on, her mother always insisted that light stay on all night long. Rapunzel found comfort in that.

"Just got in, did you?"

Her mother's voice startled her, and Rapunzel swung around, spilling a little of the water she had just poured into the tea pot.

Her mother looked weak, drawn and fragile. She also suddenly looked very old in the tattered housecoat she had worn since Rapunzel had been a little girl. She managed to walk over to the kitchen table and sit down.

"Jack and I had dinner and drinks at the pub," Rapunzel explained, feeling like a teenager again. "We lost track of time."

Her mother nodded her head and smiled. "You two always did belong together."

Rapunzel was about to protest, but her mother waved her hand in the air to stop her.

"I know what I see, more than you realize. Now how about you make some chamomile tea for both of us? Normally I detest the stuff, but tonight, well, tonight I want to have a cup of tea with my daughter."

Rapunzel tried to keep her jaw from dropping to the floor. Her mother had rarely engaged in conversations like this with her while growing up. And since she had gone away to college and begun her career, her mother had done little more than talk fluff, or criticize her actions and decisions. Every time they went beyond that, a fight ensued. As she steeped the tea bags in boiling water, she hoped tonight would not end the same way.

Bringing sugar, honey, and milk to the table, Rapunzel handed her mother her tea cup and silently sat down across from her. She didn't know what to say. The irony of her inability to communicate happening twice in one evening, when her whole job revolved around her ability to articulate, almost brought a smile to her lips. Her mother's words stopped her in her tracks.

"I'm going to be dying soon, Pun."

Rapunzel groaned inside. Not the dramatics. She didn't want to deal with those tonight, so she started to deny her mother's words.

"No, you're not. I talked to the doctor. He told me—"

Her mother held up her hand again, and Rapunzel quieted.

"The doctor told you exactly what your father and I told him to tell you and Tim. That it's just an elevated relapse, nothing critical. I know the story. But I want you to know the truth, little girl. It's time you and I cleared things up once and for all. I'm going to meet my maker with a lot of guilt on my shoulders. I don't want to carry this with me, too."

Rapunzel was confused.

"What do you mean?" she asked quietly, almost afraid to hear her mother's answer.

"I need you to hear this. You know I'm an alcoholic, honey. I have been for years. Some days I function, others I don't. And through it all your saint of a father has stuck it out with me, through the ups and downs, trying to raise you kids the best he could without me really being present," her mother explained. "But you know all that already, Pun. You always were intuitive and intelligent. And so beautiful, strong and loving. So different from me."

Tears formed in her mother's eyes, and Rapunzel couldn't help the tears that welled up in hers also.

"Why are you telling me this now, Mom?"

"Why? Two reasons. One is because I really am dying. The doctor gave me six months. And second, because I want you to know that I love you and that I'm very proud of you, girl. I admire who you've become and what you've done with your life."

Tears fell from Rapunzel's eyes. They drifted down her cheeks unencumbered, but she didn't care. Her mother was doing the same thing. Reaching out to take her hand, her mom did what she had rarely done before. She comforted her daughter, giving her hand a reassuring squeeze.

"You deserve the very best life has to offer, Pun. Everything, the whole kit and caboodle. And I want you to take it all. Don't wait around, not sure if you should, thinking you don't deserve it. That's what I did. Take this world by the horns, Pun, and ride it until the end. If you don't, you'll be sorry. Take it from me, life is too short to waste your time wallowing in self doubt and fear. That's what I did. I don't want the same fate for you."

"I live my life, Mom. I really do. I have a great life."

Her mother smiled.

"I know you do, sweetheart. All I'm saying is take some chances now and then, even if you're not sure of what lies around the next corner. Life is like one big surprise party. While that sometimes can be scary, it can also be incredibly wonderful and full of joy. You deserve that wonder and joy."

Rapunzel raised her mother's hand, laid it against her cheek and closed her eyes.

"Thank you, Mom. You're right. I need to take some chances and let down my hair."

Her mother laughed at that. The sound brought a smile to her daughter's lips. She rarely heard her mom laugh.

"You do that, sweetheart, you do that. Let down that hair of yours and live your life the way you deserve."

They continued their talk, chatting about things going on in her life, until Rapunzel noticed her mother fighting not to close her eyes.

Rapunzel walked her mother to her bed and tucked her in. She kissed her forehead and whispered in her ear.

"I love you so much, Mom."

As Rapunzel started to pull away, her mother grasped her arm.

"I love you too, honey. And don't forget. Let down that hair once in a while, and live your life, okay?"

Rapunzel smiled and nodded her head. "I will, Mom. I will." She left her mom's bedroom and went to her own.

Rapunzel didn't sleep much that night. She kept thinking about her mother's words, about Jack's words, and she knew both of them were right. It was time she starting living her life, *really* living it. And she knew just how she wanted to start doing that.

First thing the next morning, she called her office and told them she wouldn't be back for a week. Her partner, Louis, understood her need to spend extra time with her mother and told her to take all the time she needed. They would cover for her while she was gone. Next, she left a message for Jack on his voicemail. Basically, all it said was that she wanted to meet him back at the pub that night.

After that, she went shopping. It didn't take her long to find just the outfit she was looking for. After buying a pair of shoes that matched perfectly, she went to the beauty salon and had her hair, makeup and nails done. That night, after spending most of the day with her parents and brother, Rapunzel put on the new dress and shoes, touched up her hair and make up and looked in the mirror.

She couldn't believe what she was seeing.

The conservative woman Rapunzel had been had completely disappeared. In her place was a vibrantly alive woman. Her sleeveless dress was flirty and feminine, deep red with a scooped neckline and ruffled hem that settled just above the knee, and the strappy little heels were more fun than function, but they gave her legs a sexy, sleek look. The stylist had styled her hair in tousled layers that softened the angles of her face, and light makeup gave her a youthful glow. After adding a pair of gold dangly earrings, Rapunzel felt like a whole new woman—the woman she really was, confident, proud, and free to be herself.

It was only as she approached the front doors of the pub that she got nervous. What if Jack didn't show up? What if he had decided he really didn't want to deal with her issues? What if he was there, but didn't like the way she looked?

No. She wouldn't think about it. This was something she was doing for herself and herself only. It didn't matter what Jack thought. She was on a new path in her life, a path that involved living authentically, taking chances, and being proud of who she was.

Squaring her shoulders and raising her chin, she opened the front door of the pub and walked in proudly. Several men turned to stare, and Rapunzel couldn't help but feel a glow of pleasure. She scanned the room, eventually finding Jack. He was in the back corner, all the way across the room. But despite the distance, his eyes were focused on her. And from the interest in his stare, she had gotten his attention, too. His gaze remained glued to her as she made her way over to him. He stood as she got close and let out a low whistle.

"You look beautiful, Pun. The sight of you takes my breath away."

His gaze was heated, his voice low and husky. Shivers of pleasure tingled through her. It was obvious he liked what he saw.

"Thank you," she said with a shy smile. "I decided to take your advice."

Jack frowned, confusion obvious on his face.

"What advice?"

"To let down my hair. You were right. I was trying to control my life way too much, too scared to let go. Too worried about being like my mother. But after I came home last night, my mom and I had a great talk, and I realized something. I was already being like her. She hadn't lived her life careless and free, she had lived it in fear. And I don't want to live that way any longer."

Jack beamed at her and held his hand out.

"I'm glad to hear that. So how about starting right now?"

Now it was her turn to be confused.

"What do you mean?"

"Dance with me."

Rapunzel's heart sped up and she caught her breath. This was it. Now or never. Time to live. Taking his hand, she let Jack lead her out to the little dance floor in the middle of the pub. Suddenly, Josh Turner's song, *Would You Go With Me,* began to play on the jukebox. Smiling, she stepped into Jack's arms.

Rapunzel was ready this time. She was ready to fly with

Jack, ready to take a chance on him, and on life.
She was ready to let down her hair.

The End

Eden Robins loves writing paranormal, futuristic and fantasy romances. She enjoys creating dark, dangerous and decadent tales with unexpected twists, complex characters and love affairs that lead to that wonderful happily ever after. With the success of her futuristic *Tomorrow* trilogy and *After Sundown* fantasy series Eden is firmly entrenched in the world of Science Fiction, Fantasy and Paranormal Romance.

Please visit Eden's website at www.edenrobins.com
Stop by her Facebook page or send her a note at edenrobins@gmail.com.

A Modern Dancing Princess

Janet Miller
aka Cricket Starr

Chapter One

Ryan O'Toole had seen a lot of distraught parents in his checkered career as a private detective but he had to admit this dad was one for the books. Not that there was anything about the man himself that was particularly unusual.

Paul Nuell was at first sight exactly what he seemed to be. Slightly overweight but very well dressed, he was a gentleman whose age fell in that comfortable place between youth and elderly with money enough to indulge whatever inclinations he had and the common sense to not let it go to his head.

From the research Ryan had done after Mr. Nuell had called for an appointment, the man was a businessman with dealings in several industries and was well respected by all. Scrupulously honest himself, Ryan always researched his clients to make sure they weren't going to ask him to do anything that would violate his sense of ethics.

But his client wanted nothing illegal. What made Mr. Nuell seek him out was that he was the parent of a daughter at that age where she became more a worry than a pleasure, so it wasn't surprising the man had decided to consult a detective to find out what his offspring was up to. Nothing unusual about that.

What was strange was the man's story. That was unusual.

"My daughter is as sweet as a girl could be," Nuell said. "I have no worries about her as a whole. Because I insist, she lives in my house and I'm sure like most girls at her age she'd rather be on her own. Even so, she's respectful and thoughtful. Keeps her curfew and does well in college. No odd boyfriends or odd vices. All in all she's a delight to have around."

"Then I fail to see the problem," Ryan said. "Why consult me?"

Mr. Nuell waved his hand. "It's the shoes, you see, Mr. O'Toole. Her handmade designer dancing shoes that she has specially made for her by Maliogunter."

Attention caught, Ryan leaned forward. "Maliogunter, the reclusive fashion designer? He only makes a few pair of shoes a year. Those most cost a fortune!"

If were really possible for a man to wring his hands, Nuell would be wringing his. "Oh, Mr. O'Toole, you have it right on the money. They do cost a fortune. They are beautiful shoes and I have no issue with them…but she wears them out in a single night."

Even Ryan found that hard to believe. "In one night? Wears them out? That's ridiculous. You should buy more durable shoes."

"I wish it were that simple but it isn't." Nuell shook his head. "My Crissy can only wear the best. Her feet are very delicate. Maliougunter was my daughter's first dance instructor and he designed these shoes for her. They are made just for her and to her express measurements."

Normally Ryan liked to keep a neutral expression but this time he couldn't avoid his look of disbelief. "Even so… a shoe that wears out in one night of dancing?"

"But that's the mystery, Mr. O'Toole. That's why I've come to consult you. It isn't really the expense."

"No?"

"No, not really." Ryan saw the worry in the man's face and it troubled him. Nuell didn't look like a man to whom worry came naturally.

"The thing is," Nuell said. "I can't for the life of me understand what she is doing to wear out her shoes so quickly. She doesn't leave the house…as far as anyone can tell she's in her room all night but in the morning the soles of her dancing shoes are worn paper-thin. How is it happening?"

The portly man shook his head in wonderment. "I'm afraid something is happening to her and that it could be dangerous."

Ryan leaned back in his chair. "You are sure of this?"

"Sure as I can be about anything. I tell you, it is a mystery. Please say you can help us." Nuell looked like he was ready to beg.

For a few long moments Ryan studied the grain of the wood of his desk. Like the rest of the furniture it needed polishing, the result of not being able to hire a regular cleaning person. There really wasn't much money in being a private detective if you were an honest man—which he was. Here was a way to make some decent money if he could solve the mystery.

He'd always loved a mystery—as much as he loved a good fairy tale. Which made him think of a story from his childhood that Nuell's tale resembled.

Ryan laughed. "Hm… reminds me of that fairy tale about the twelve dancing princesses. Every night they wore out their dancing slippers until the king found a soldier to follow them and find out what they were up to."

Mr. Nuell stared at him, then visibly blanched. "Twelve princesses? Oh good heavens. For once I'm glad Crissy is an only child—otherwise I'd go bankrupt replacing shoes."

Ryan laughed again. "Mr. Nuell, I'm intrigued by your story. If you want me, I'm on the case."

The portly man leapt to his feet and grabbed his hand, shaking it firmly. "Oh thank you, Mr. O'Toole. I'm in your debt. If you can solve this I'll pay you whatever you ask."

On first glance Crissy Nuell was the sweetest girl a man could hope to meet. She looked at Ryan and smiled, all glossy brown hair and bright hazel eyes and with skin a delicate shade of tan that only someone with a lot of time on their hands could acquire.

That tan looked really good on her.

She looked like the million bucks she was supposed to be

worth and then some. But even more…she appeared to be a really sweet kid. The kind of girl that a man might fall in love with if he weren't careful. Which would be a really bad idea Ryan quickly decided given that he was who he was and she wasn't someone he had any business falling for.

But then she looked at him with those bright hazel eyes, caught somewhere between blue and green and he had trouble remembering what business he was in. He bet her eye color was changeable with her mood. Her mood this afternoon was apprehensive…eyes erring on the side of green.

She folded her hands and "I wish I knew what to tell you, Mr. O'Toole. I just have no idea what is happening to my shoes."

"No idea at all? After all, Ms. Nuell, they were on your feet weren't they?"

"I suppose they must have been," she admitted. "My feet are always very sore in the morning and I'm exhausted all the time. I must be wearing them out. But if I am, I don't know how it is happening. I go to bed each night and can't remember a thing in the morning."

"Do you sleep-walk?"

She looked honestly perplexed. "Maybe, but no one has ever seen me do it. Perhaps I'm dancing in my sleep. That would explain why I couldn't remember."

Ryan looked into her eyes and fell a little deeper into their depths. Shaking his head he pulled out and tried another tack. "Have you ever tried simply not ordering more shoes? Perhaps if you didn't have a fresh pair you wouldn't wear them out."

She sighed and its sincerity echoed deep into Ryan's soul. "I have tried that…but it was no use. Somehow I'm ordering the new shoes online during the night. Even taking my computer off the Internet and locking it in my father's safe before going to bed didn't help."

"You ordered the shoes after you retired…but not on your computer?"

Those big greenish-blue eyes stared into him. "That's the truth."

"Have you tried talking to the man you're ordering them

from, Maliougunter to find out how they are being ordered?"

A delicate blush tinged her cheeks. "I don't want to talk to him."

That was interesting. "Why not? You keep ordering these expensive shoes from him."

"It's hard to explain. We were close once. He taught me to dance and even helped me with some other things."

"Like what?"

Her blush deepened. "Well, can you keep a secret?"

"Maybe. If it isn't something your father should know."

"Oh it isn't. It's just that I used to bite my nails." She held out her hands to display ten perfectly shaped fingernails. "I tried everything to quit and it all failed. But he was able to get me to stop in one try."

Crissy sounded like she'd had a crush on her former dance instructor. That didn't appeal to him but he had to admit her nails looked great. "So why don't you want to talk to him?"

Her gaze dropped to her hands and she sighed. "I just don't think it's a good idea to involve him. We had a kind of falling out."

"And yet you order expensive shoes from him?"

Crissy sighed again. "I know it sounds crazy...but this whole thing is crazy."

"Crazy...or a fairy tale," Ryan acknowledged. He reached forward to take her hand. "I'm willing to believe you. But I have to see this happen for myself."

Her hand was small and delicate in his. Her smile couldn't help but charm. "I love my father and I hate that this is distressing him, Mr. O'Toole. I'll cooperate as much as I can. Will you stay tonight outside my room?"

Ryan smiled. "I'll be happy to."

Chapter Two

"So, Mr. O'Toole, what have you got to say for yourself?" Mr. Nuell was furious and Ryan had to admit, he had a right to be.

"There isn't much I can say, sir. Last night your daughter managed to wear out her shoes again and then this morning a new pair was delivered." Ryan shook his head in bewilderment. "I can't understand how it happened though. I was sitting on a chair right outside her bedroom door the entire time."

Nuell groaned. "I'm afraid that has been the story all along. Every time I've stationed someone in the hall outside her door she's managed to get by them. She must be either dancing in her room or leaving some other way."

Ryan studied his fingernails. They needed attention but a manicure wasn't part of his budget this month…truth was the rent on his office had barely made the cut. He didn't need to lose this job.

"She isn't dancing in her room," he said. "I was outside the door all night and I'd have heard her moving about. Plus she's ordering new shoes every night and I personally confiscated her computer before she went to bed." He shook his head. "Somehow she must be leaving the premises."

"My daughter is sneaking out of the house?" Nuell looked distraught. "You have to admit Mr. O'Toole, that can't be good.

More is at stake here than expensive shoes."

"It isn't good. What is worse is that she claims not to remember it happening…and I believe her."

Ryan couldn't explain why he believed Crissy was somehow innocent, but he did. When he'd confronted her this morning with the telltale worn-out shoes, she'd burst into tears.

"Please Mr. O'Toole," she'd said. "I swear I don't know what happened. The last thing I remembered was lying in my bed, and then this morning the shoes were on the floor all worn out."

She was just too sincere to be lying. Without thinking, Ryan gathered her into his arms and let her cry on his shoulder. At first he'd held her because she needed comforting but then he kept holding her because it felt too good not to.

Crissy seemed to like being in his arms as well. When she'd finally stopped sobbing she'd gazed up at him with that sweet pinkness in her cheeks. Reluctantly he'd let her go but she hadn't moved too far from him.

"I guess I shouldn't have done that," he'd told her. "Not very professional of me to grab you like that."

She smiled then. "I didn't mind. I think I like having your arms around me, Mr. O'Toole. I like you."

He liked her too. "You should call me Ryan if you mean that."

"I mean it. And you should call me Crissy, Ryan." Her smile broadened as she tried his name out. "I like that too. I've never known a man like you. You seem…honest."

"I like to think that I am."

She glanced down at her hands again. "I'm honest too. Mr. O'Toole, I mean, Ryan. I don't know what is happening to me."

And just like that he believed her. Whatever was happening it wasn't her fault. He'd bet his last nickel on it— which would be the entirety of his savings account if he didn't get to the bottom of this mystery.

He thought again about that story about the twelve dancing princesses. They drugged their watcher with a sleeping draught mixed with wine and would sneak out through a secret passage. Crissy hadn't given him anything to drink and he hadn't slept so he was sure she wasn't leaving by the door to her room.

But that left the possibility of a secret passageway. Either there was a hidden exit in her room or perhaps she used a more mundane exit—her bedroom window that opened onto the street.

Ryan decided he would watch another night…but this time while he'd pretend to be in the hallway outside Crissy's room he'd really be in the street where he could watch her bedroom window.

Later that night Ryan was parked on the street outside the house when he noticed a cab waiting half a block away. Leaving his car he wandered by it as unobtrusively as possible and saw the man staring up at Crissy's bedroom window. He quickly moved back to his car to wait.

After a while a slim figure slipped out of the window and shimmied down the drainpipe to the sidewalk and headed for the cab. Even from his position Ryan made out the short black skirt, bright pink tank top, patterned hose and distinctive dancing shoes on her feet. It looked like Crissy was dressed up to go dancing.

His heart sank a little at the sight. She really had been lying to him.

Ryan watched the cab until it went past him and then he turned the ignition and pulled out after it. In the back seat of the cab he saw Crissy's distinctive profile and his heart sank lower.

When he'd seen her earlier she'd worn a conservative blouse and slacks and then when he'd confiscated her computer she'd been dressed in a flannel nightgown with small pink roses. His modern princess was deceiving him and her father, apparently a willing part in this shoe-leather wearing out adventure. Ryan had hoped that somehow she was an innocent victim but it was not to be.

He followed as the cab moved swiftly through the late night city traffic to the parking lot of a small nightclub.

Ryan checked out the unguarded doorway as he parked his car. Apparently this place was so exclusive it didn't even need a velvet rope or a bouncer. If you weren't part of its crowd you didn't even know this place existed. Crissy emerged from the cab and headed inside while the driver sought a place to wait nearby.

Leaving his vehicle, Ryan went to the doorway and took a peek. Inside was dark but the music pounded in a heavy beat that set his feet to tapping. Good dancing music.

Good music to wear out a pair of shoes to.

He went in and saw the open dance floor, a few people moving to the beat. One of them was Crissy in her bright pink top whirling and twirling with wild abandon. There was a man dancing with her, occasionally grabbing her and pulling her close. She didn't seem to like him touching her, pulling away as soon as she could, but he didn't let up.

It was all Ryan could do to not charge onto the floor, seize the man and throw him against the wall, but he forced himself to wait. Before he revealed himself he needed to know what was really going on. Part of him still hoped that there was an explanation for Crissy's behavior other than treachery.

He made himself invisible in a dark corner of the club and kept watch. After a while, Crissy left the floor accompanied by her dance partner, moving to a table not too far away.

She sat heavily on one of the chairs, clearly exhausted. "I don't know why you are doing this to me," she wailed and her distress was so heartfelt Ryan couldn't help but feel it.

The man she'd been dancing with sat opposite her. He wasn't terribly tall but he looked fit, his dark pants and shirt clinging to his frame. His dark greasy looking hair fell long over his narrow face and his dark eyes glittered malevolently. Even his skinny mustache looked villainous.

"Because I can. Because I must…it is an imperative. You refused me…me, Maliougunter, the greatest dance instructor in the world. You refused to marry me, then you refused to be my student any longer, even after I created my greatest dance shoe for you."

"But I don't want to be a dancer any more. That's why I'm

going to college to get my teaching degree. As for marrying you…" she hesitated. "That's why I said I didn't want to see you anymore. I don't love you and I never could."

"I know. That's why I make you buy my shoes anyway. If I can't have you, I will at least have the money you spend on my shoes." Maliougunter looked triumphant.

With a low moan Crissy shook her head. "Why can't I stop this? Why can't I remember where I've been in the morning?"

Maliougunter's laugh sounded evil. "Because in addition to being a great dancer, and a great shoe designer, I am also a great hypnotist, my dear. Remember how I made you quit chewing your nails?" He leaned over the table and smiled wickedly at her. "When I was curing you of that I also made it impossible for you to disobey me."

But then the man looked frustrated. "My suggestion should have made you fall in love with me so I could marry you but it didn't work that way."

Crissy looked at him wearily. "I couldn't love you. I didn't think I could love anyone…" She broke off but her companion noticed.

"So, you think you could fall in love with that detective your father hired?" he scoffed. "That is ridiculous."

Crissy lifted her head and even though Ryan could see she was beyond weary, something inside her rose to the challenge. "Why couldn't I fall in love with him? I like him and he likes me. Mr. O'Toole is an honest man which is more than I could say for you, Bob."

"Don't call me that," the other man growled.

"Why not. It is your real name, *Bob*. It is what you were called before you changed it." Suddenly she smiled. "I remember Mr. O'Toole, and now I remember everything else. I remembered that you tricked me into letting you hypnotize me and that you've been controlling me every night. I don't think I'll forget where I've been tomorrow morning and I don't think I'll be coming here any more. You've lost your power over me."

She rose to her feet. "I'm not going to dance with you any more. I'm not going to order more shoes."

"You will." Bob looked smug. "After all, you can't leave

here until your shoes are worn out and a new pair ordered."
He gestured to a computer positioned nearby, the monitor
glowing in the dark. "Until you order a new pair the cab won't
take you home."

Crissy lifted her head higher. "I'll walk home if I must."
She turned to leave but Maliougunter seized her arm and
dragged her closer.

"You'll leave when I let you."

Ryan left the dark corner he'd hidden in. "I think you
should let the lady go."

Chapter Three

Maliougunter swung to face him. "If it isn't the honest detective...what are you doing here?" he sneered.

"Rescuing a lady it seems." Drawing back a fist he let it fly into Maliougunter's face. The man staggered back with blood streaming from his no longer perfectly aligned nose and Ryan grabbed Crissy's arm.

She stared up at him, joy mixed with apprehension in her eyes. "Please get me out of here," she whispered.

Ryan didn't need to hear more. He hustled her out of the club to the street and to his car parked outside. He pushed Crissy into the passenger seat before moving to the driver's side. Starting the car he was able to pull out before Maliougunter appeared in the doorway.

They left the man helplessly shouting after them, holding his bloody nose.

Crissy leaned back into the worn upholstery of his car and closed her eyes. After a while a pair of loose tears trickled down her cheeks.

"Why are you crying?" Ryan asked.

"Because you must hate me. You are a good man who values honesty and now you know that I've been deceiving you and my father."

Ryan shook his head. "That wasn't how I see it. Did you

actually know during the day that you were doing this at night?" He glanced at her outfit. "He said he hypnotized you to make you obey him. I believe that to be true. You aren't even dressed like the Crissy I met yesterday."

She glanced down at what she was wearing and was quiet a long time. "I guess you're right. I didn't know what I was doing. It was like a dream. During the day I couldn't remember anything." She gave him a cautious look. "I didn't remember at night either until he mentioned you. Then I thought about how nice you were to me today even though I'd worn out my shoes again…"

Even in the dim light of the car, he thought she blushed.

"Thinking of me made you remember who you were and what was really going on?"

"Something like that. I think Bob's influence over me is finally broken."

Ryan smiled. "That's what I heard. That was quite a speech you made tonight."

She leaned forward and undid the straps to her shoes. Lifting them she glared at the worn through soles. "I am never wearing these again…nor any pair like them." Opening the window she tossed them into the street.

Ryan watched her for a long moment. "You know, I like to dance."

"You do?" She turned her head to gaze at him.

"Yep. I was hoping to dance at my wedding but to do that I'll need a bride."

He could almost hear the corners of her mouth turning up when she spoke. "Why would you have a problem finding a bride?"

"I don't have a lot of money. Hard to propose to a woman without it."

Crissy seemed to consider that. "I'm not interested in a person's wealth. What I want is a man with integrity. That's even rarer than money."

She tilted her head at him. "My father said he'd pay you anything you asked. You're going to get a big reward for stopping Bob and rescuing me. Suppose you asked for something more?"

"More?"

"Well, yes. To start with I'm sure my father needs a man he can trust to investigate his business deals before he commits himself. That would be pretty profitable for you."

Ryan couldn't help his grin. A fat retainer from Crissy's father would solve his financial difficulties. "I'll have to suggest that to your father now that I've cracked this case."

Crissy nodded her head. "Of course there is still the matter of the bride."

He gave her a quick glance. "That is still a problem. Any ideas in that area?"

She shrugged shyly. "Suppose you asked me to be your wife?"

Ryan pulled the car over to the curb and stopped. "You know what you are saying? After all, we haven't even kissed yet, what makes you think that we'd even be good together as a couple?"

Crissy leaned over to him and let her lips brush against his, once, then twice. Ryan put his arms around her and pulled her close and this time when their lips met they stayed together and the kiss got serious.

By the time it ended they were staring into each other's eyes.

"Well," Crissy said. "I guess that settles that. We're compatible."

Ryan couldn't help his smile. That was the way the fairy tale of the twelve dancing princesses ended, with the soldier married to one of the king's daughters. "We should probably date a bit first and see where things are in a few months. But are you sure you're willing think about getting serious about me, Crissy? Even with your dad's business I won't be able to afford expensive dancing shoes."

She leaned closer and leaned her head up for him to kiss her again. "Oh, Ryan. With you I'd be happy to dance barefoot."

The End

Janet Miller aka Cricket Starr is a mild-mannered software engineer who writes code and design documents, but at night and on weekends she turns to the creation of offbeat stories about imaginary pasts, presents, and futures for Ellora's Cave, New Concepts Publishing, and Red Sage.

You can read more about Janet's books at her website: http://www.janetmillerromance.com

Grandma's House

(Little Red Riding Hood)

Joy Nash

My dearest granddaughter,

Though we have never met, I feel I know you. We are one blood, and for a Scot, blood is everything. Family and clan count more than physical distance, or years of silence—yes, even more than pride. I discarded that cold comfort long ago, when I begged your mother to bring you home. How I longed to know you! Hold you. Watch you grow.

Sadly, my Maris refused to return to me. Now she is gone, so suddenly, and my hope of reconciliation has died with her. But you, my precious child, are very much alive. I pray you will cross the ocean between us and come to me...

Tasha MacLeod folded the crisp white stationary bearing her grandmother's impeccable penmanship, and slipped it carefully into the front pocket of her backpack. Sliding down on the slick leather seat, she jammed her fists into the pockets of her red sweatshirt hoodie and stared at the lush greenery streaming by the limousine window. Rolling pastures. Fluffy white cotton-ball sheep. Cloud-strewn sky. If not for the occasional forbidding castle, she might have been home in Vermont.

Scotland. She was actually in Scotland. An uneasy thrill ping-ponged around in her stomach. It wasn't that she was afraid, exactly. More like *confused*. Tasha's mother had rarely mentioned her birth country or her family there, but when she had, she hadn't disguised her bitterness. And she'd always used the past tense. Tasha had grown up thinking her grandmother was dead.

Until a month or so after the funeral, when the letter came from a Lady Rossalyn MacLeod of Scotland. Her grandmother. Perfectly legit, Mama's lawyer had told Tasha—he'd investigated, and the woman's identity was what she claimed it to be. Tasha, who hadn't known any family other than her mother, had been seized by a fierce curiosity. And, if truth be told, more than a little resentment. Why hadn't her mother ever told her they weren't alone in the world?

So here Tasha was, on a trip to grandma's house. It sounded so quaint. So cozy. So *comfortable*. Or at least it had until a Rolls Royce limo, complete with taciturn, white-gloved driver, had met her plane in Edinburgh. She stretched out her legs. There was so much room, her feet didn't reach the opposite seat. She'd grown up in public housing; until Mama's funeral, she'd never ridden in a limousine in her life. And that one had been nothing like this. Her seatbelt seemed wholly inadequate for how adrift she felt.

The limo glided through a village. A quaint cluster of cottages and shops flashed by, and then they were in the countryside again. She jabbed the intercom button. The driver, who'd squelched every conversational gambit Tasha had attempted in the last five hours, glanced into the rear view mirror.

"Aye, Miss MacLeod?"

"How much farther?"

"We're already on MacLeod land, Miss. The village we just passed belongs to the estate." Decelerating, he executed a wide right turn between a pair of massive stone pillars. "Just a mile or so to the main house, now."

A mile on a narrow twisting drive, through dense forest. Ten minutes later, Tasha choked back a hysterical laugh as the forest gave way to a wide expanse of manicured lawn that would have done any golf course proud. She blinked. House, had the driver said? More like a freaking castle. Solid and gray, the ancient structure set on a gentle rise of land came complete with turrets. The grassy depression ringing it even looked like it had once been a moat.

The limo glided past a pair of sleek Mercedes sedans, then

came to a halt before a massive arched doorway topped by a carved family crest. Swallowing became very difficult. Rossalyn—Tasha had trouble calling the woman 'grandmother' in her mind—had to be richer than God. Mama had traded *this* for a life of near poverty in a foreign country? It was unbelievable. Barely eighteen when Tasha was born, scraping by on her wages as a cleaning lady, Maris had scarcely managed to feed and clothe herself and her daughter. More often than not during her childhood, Tasha had gone to bed hungry. Never once during all that time had Mama hinted she'd come from money.

The limo driver exited the vehicle and rounded the hood, on his way to Tasha's door. That kind of servant stuff creeped Tasha out. Grabbing her backpack and the pathetic gingham-trimmed gift basket of Vermont maple fudge and preserves that had seemed like a good idea at the time, Tasha hopped out of the limo under her own steam.

A recent rain had turned the stone pavement into a slippery charcoal black mirror. Steadying herself with one hand on the car door, she turned away from the driver's quiet disapproval.

And that's when she saw it. A black wolf, standing at the forest's edge, less than fifty feet away. A slanting ray of the late afternoon sun glinted yellow on its eyes.

The animal bared its teeth. A low growl erupted from its throat. The sound seemed to vibrate, not in Tasha's ears, but in her mind.

Panic flashed through her, leaving her face flushed and her hands ice cold. She couldn't breathe. Couldn't look away from the creature. It was huge, much larger than any dog. And it was looking right at her.

The driver reached her side; Tasha horrified him by clutching at his arm.

His gruff Scots accent seemed very far away. "Miss MacLeod? What is it? Are ye ill?"

She looked up at him. "That...wolf. It won't...attack, will it?"

"Wolf?" His tone sharpened. "What wolf?"

She lifted a finger, pointing. She was trembling like an aspen leaf. "The one over th..."

Her words died in her throat. The wolf was gone.

"'T'was a dog," the driver said. "Nothing more."

Tasha swallowed hard. A dog. Of course. She lowered her hand, struggling to inhale around the clenched fist in her chest. "I...jet lag, I guess."

"Of course, miss."

And then a female voice called her name, and all thoughts of the wolf fled.

"Natasha."

An elegant elderly woman, costumed in a fashionable wool suit, emerged from the arched doorway, the heels of her suede boots clicking as she glided toward Tasha. Her blond hair, shot through with white, reflected the dying sunlight.

"Grandmother?" The word felt thick on Tasha's tongue.

"Oh, my dear, dear lass."

Tasha found herself enfolded tightly in Rossalyn's arms. When her grandmother drew back, tears were glistening in her vivid blue eyes. She held Tasha at arms length, searching her face intently.

"At last, you're here," she said softly. She smiled. "Oh, how I have prayed for this day."

Awkwardly, Tasha pressed the gift basket into Rossalyn's hands. "Um...I brought you this."

"How thoughtful, my dear." Rossalyn handed the basket off to the driver. "Here...leave your rucksack for Angus as well, there's a good lass. Tea will be laid in the drawing room shortly. Although," she added, frowning slightly as she took in Tasha's red hoodie sweatshirt and faded jeans for the first time, "you might wish to change into something less...casual. But no," she decided in an abrupt reversal of tone and purpose that left Tasha's head spinning. "Hunter's expected at the office for a late meeting. Tea cannot wait."

"Hunter?" Tasha asked.

"My right hand man at MacLeod Textiles. A most capable lad. Distant kin, actually." She cocked her head. "Let me see...Hunter would be your fifth cousin twice removed, I

84

believe. Top in his class at Oxford, and a fine rugby player besides. One couldn't ask for better."

"I see," Tasha said cautiously.

Rossalyn linked her arm through Tasha's and guided her under the arched portal into an open castle forecourt. A profusion of roses was just coming into bloom. Beyond the garden, a doorman bowed them into a dark-paneled entry hall, then looked at Tasha expectantly.

"Fergus will take your jacket, my dear," Rossalyn prompted.

"Oh." Tasha unzipped her hoodie and shrugged it into the man's waiting hands.

Her left shirt sleeve caught, hiking up her arm. Before Tasha could adjust it, Rossalyn frowned and caught Tasha's hand. Turning it palm upward, she exposed a vivid red circle, about the size of a quarter, on Tasha's wrist.

"Why, my dear, whatever happened? Did you burn yourself?"

Cheeks burning, Tasha tugged her wrist from her grandmother's grasp. "No. It's not a burn. It's a birthmark."

"Truly? It looks so...raw. And painful."

"It's always been there," Tasha said, shoving down her sleeve. And its appearance had always bothered her. It looked like someone had branded her with a hot iron. It was the reason she rarely wore short sleeves. "It's no big deal. It doesn't hurt at all."

But the mark tingled sometimes. The sensation started now, tiny needle points dancing on her skin. She resisted the urge to rub them away.

"A good dermatologist could remove it, perhaps," Rossalyn said.

"Probably." Tasha would've had it done already, if she'd had the money.

Rossalyn was silent for a moment, then she once again took Tasha's arm. "Come. Hunter is waiting."

She steered Tasha through a large room filled with heavy, brooding furniture and dark, glowering oil paintings. Lighting was dim, giving Tasha the impression she'd been caught in a museum after closing hours. A set of double doors gave way into a smaller, more cheerful room.

One end of a comfortably worn leather couch held the most sinfully gorgeous man Tasha had ever seen in her life.

The young Adonis rose as they entered. God, but was he tall. Six-four, at least. He wore business attire—charcoal gray suit, crisp white shirt, red silk tie. His fair hair reflected the light from the wall sconce behind him, forming a sort of halo about his head.

"Hunter," Rossalyn said, smiling. "May I present my granddaughter. Tasha MacLeod."

Hunter inclined his golden head. "Tasha. It's a pleasure." His Scots accent was faint, his speech carrying more of a British flavor.

"Um...thank you," she said, then shut her eyes briefly. Apparently, the part of her brain dedicated to composing witty conversation had shut down. But then, a handsome man tended to do that to her. Especially when he wore a thousand-dollar suit opposite her thrift store jeans.

Rossalyn perched herself elegantly on an armchair, waving Tasha to the sofa next to Hunter. Feeling like a grubby duck, Tasha sank into the soft leather. A uniformed maid appeared, carrying a laden tea tray. Tasha suddenly remembered how hungry she was.

Hunter flashed her a smile. Tasha's heart stuttered. The man was gorgeous enough with a serious expression; with a grin he was downright lethal.

"Jet-lagged?" he asked.

"A little."

"Horrid things, planes." Rossalyn gave a delicate shudder as she sipped her tea. "I will never step foot on one."

"It was my first time on an airplane," Tasha confessed.

"Really?" Hunter said. "I'll have to take you up in the corporate jet."

He bit into a triangle of shortbread, somehow managing to consume the pastry without a single crumb falling in his lap. Tasha was not quite as adept.

Conversation turned to business. MacLeod Textiles, Tasha

gathered, was a major exporter of Scottish wool. Hence the acres and acres of sheep pasture she'd passed on the way here.

"Have you worked for my grandmother a long time?" Tasha asked.

Hunter grinned at Rossalyn, who returned his regard with a motherly smile. "More than twenty years. I was a lad of nine when I first came to MacLeod Castle. Rossalyn took me in when my father died. Your grandmother taught me everything I know about the wool business."

"Perhaps that was true once," Rossalyn put in with a light laugh. "But Hunter left me behind years ago. He's made the business what it is today."

"Our wool is the finest in Scotland," Hunter said. "We have a chain of stores here in the U.K., but a good portion of our business is in exports. Every fleece we process comes from our own sheep, born and raised here on the estate."

"You do have a lot of sheep," Tasha said. "Must be hard to keep the wolf from the door."

Rossalyn's chin jerked up. "What did you say? What wolf?"

Tasha's eyes widened. "I...no wolf. It was just a joke. Because I thought I saw a dog on the driveway..."

Hunter's brows came down. "Impossible. We don't keep dogs."

"Perhaps...perhaps it was a stray." Rossalyn's tone was strained. She exchanged a glance with Hunter, whose lips thinned.

"What did the animal look like?" Hunter asked, his gaze intent.

"Um...big, black. Shaggy. It kind of looked like a wolf. But honestly, I don't even know if I really saw it. It was there and gone in a second. I might have imagined the whole thing."

"Maybe," Hunter said.

But he didn't seem convinced.

"Well? What do you think?"
"What I think hardly matters. Does she have the mark?"
"She does. Just as I suspected."

"She can't know what it means. If she did, she would never have mentioned the wolf."

"That beast is bold, to come so close."

"He wants her."

"Of course. But she is ours. He will not have her."

It was still dark when Tasha sat up in bed, wide awake. A glance at her watch, glowing softly on the night table, revealed the time as three a.m. Ten p.m. at home and the start of her shift at the hospital, where she worked as a nurse's aid. Giving up on sleep, she swung her legs over the edge of the mattress. The darn thing was so high off the ground that a wrong turn in the night could result in permanent injury.

The second floor room Rossalyn had given her overlooked the grounds behind the castle. A damp sweet breeze wafted through the open casement. The moon, just shy of full, hung as a round, hazy ball above a shadow-strewn terraced garden. Wisps of fog curled on the neat gravel pathways.

Her birthmark tingled. She rubbed it, aware of a growing need to be out under the sky. Could she find her way to a back door? She'd give it a try, anyway. Dressing quickly, she grabbed her red hoodie—it'd been neatly hung in an antique wardrobe by unseen hands, and slipped quietly down the carpeted stairway.

Fifteen minutes and a few false turns later, Tasha stepped into cool, damp air and inhaled deeply. Moonlight painted the garden in liquid silver, giving the mist curling about her ankles an otherworldly glow. Hidden birds called the dawn. She moved down the path, away from the castle. It was like walking on a cloud. Or into a dream.

She made her way, glided between two long rows of planting beds, filled with budding roses, arching lilacs, and a myriad of other blooms she couldn't name. A long arbor of trellised vines arced over a moonshine-dappled path, beckoning like a tunnel to a fairy world. She stepped into the archway.

The semicircle of light at the other end framed a large canine figure.

Her breath left her. The animal was no figment of her imagination. The black wolf was as real as she was. The enormous creature lifted its head. Its eyes glinted gold in the moonlight.

She should have been terrified. She should have backed away. She didn't. Amazingly, the wolf didn't repel; it fascinated. Her chest felt strange, as if her ribcage was expanding and contracting at the same time. Anticipation wound a spring in her belly.

The voice, when it came, was a faint vibration in her mind. *Come to me, lass.*

Entranced, she started toward the beast, her footsteps soft on the gravel path. For a moment, it just stood, watching. Then, turning, it loped out of view. A sudden, inexplicable sense of loss sliced through Tasha's heart.

"No!"

She broke into a run. But when she arrived, panting, at the other end of the long arbor, the wolf was nowhere to be seen.

Her birthmark sparkled. She spun around, searching the shadows. "Come back!"

She held her breath and strained her ears, listening. Nothing. Her heartbeat slowed to normal, some measure of sanity returning. What the hell was she doing, chasing after a large, stray dog in the dark? She was lucky the thing hadn't turned and lunged.

An early dawn was breaking. Sighing, she turned around, prepared to make her way back to the castle. Until she looked up and saw a man standing ten paces in front of her, blocking her path.

The first thought that registered in her startled brain was that the stranger was wearing a kilt. Her second thought was that he looked damn good in it.

His kilt was a simple green and blue tartan belted at his waist and diagonally sashed over his broad, white shirted chest. His dark hair, longish and slightly tangled, curled at his jaw. He wasn't handsome—not like Hunter, in any case, but there was something compelling in his expression. Something that made Tasha take a step toward him, before she realized what she was doing and stopped.

He moved toward her on silent feet. Abruptly, sanity intruded on the spell he'd seemed to cast about her. She had no idea who he was, or what he wanted.

She fought the urge to turn and bolt—she sensed he could outrun her in a heartbeat. Would a scream bring help fast enough, if the need arose? She had to hope that it would. In the meantime, she'd just act as if the stranger was harmless, and hope like hell it was true.

She cleared her throat. He halted, barely three steps away. Close enough for her to feel the heat radiating from his body. She tilted her head back to get a better look at his face, noticing his eyes for the first time. They were light brown, almost golden. Intelligent. Soulful. Without doubt the most beautiful eyes she'd ever seen.

"Hello." She was unaccountably breathless.

He nodded. "Good morn, lass."

His Scots burr was rough, lingering like a caress. So unlike Hunter's clipped, British-tinged tone. Though why she had the urge to compare the two men, she couldn't say.

"Did you see a dog here in the garden?" she asked suddenly. "A big black one? No collar."

Amusement gleamed in his eyes. "A dog, lass?"

"Well, it looked almost like a wolf, but of course, that's ridiculous. He was over by the arbor. Is he yours?"

His lips curved. "Nay lass. I know him, though. Goes where he will, that one."

"A stray?"

"He willna hurt ye."

She eased forward a step, hinting she wanted to pass. He didn't seem to be inclined to move out of the way. She stopped.

"Do you work here?" she asked. "In the gardens?"

His smile widened. "I'm no gardener, if that's what ye mean." He inclined his head. "I'm Kieran MacDonald." He paused. "I live in the village."

Her shoulders relaxed, marginally. A neighbor, not a vagrant. "Kieran," she said cautiously. "That's a nice name. I'm..."

"Tasha MacLeod."

Her brows shot up. "How did you know?"

"How many American granddaughters do ye imagine Rossalyn MacLeod has?"

She smiled sheepishly. "Just the one, I guess. I suppose everyone in the village knows about my visit?"

"As they know of your mother's recent death," he said quietly. "'Tis sorry I am for your loss."

Tasha's throat threatened to close. "Thank you."

"She was a beautiful lass, your mother. Kind, as well. Her eyes were always laughing."

She couldn't help but stare. "You knew her?"

"Aye. She was ten years older than me, but I worshipped her. Almost as much as your father did."

Her head grew light. "You knew my father, too?"

"Why of course. He was a MacDonald as well, though not a close kin."

"What...what was his name? His first name, I mean."

His brow creased. "Ye do not know?"

Tasha shook her head. "I don't know anything about my father. Only that he died before my mother left for America. Mama...she never spoke of him. Didn't have a picture. And she wouldn't even tell me his name."

Kieran was silent for a moment. "Ewan," he said at last. "Ewan Artur MacDonald."

"Ewan." She repeated the syllables softly. "Thank you. I never understood why Mama wouldn't talk of him. She would only say it was better if I didn't know anything. Safer."

"Aye. Most likely it was. But ye are no longer a child."

She looked up sharply. "What do you mean by that? What do you know of him? What was he like? How did he die?"

His jaw set. "Ewan was a fine lad. Bold, brave. He loved Maris more than life itself. As for how he died..." He let out a breath. "Aye, I remember it well. He was murdered."

"Murdered?" Tasha was aghast. "By who?"

Kieran grimaced. "'Twas a long time ago, lass. Perhaps 'tis better to leave it be." He paused. "Ye have the look of him, ye know. His hair was as black as yours."

She touched her cheek. "I thought that might be the case. My mother was fair, and Rossalyn is as well."

"Ye have Ewan's eyes, as well. And his way of moving." Suddenly, he reached out and captured her wrist. "Forgive me, lass. I must know..."

She stood transfixed, stunned by the sudden heat of his fingertips on her skin. He turned her left hand palm upward and pushed back the sleeve of her sweatshirt.

Air hissed through his teeth. "*Mo Dhia*. I dared to hope, but I never truly dreamed..."

He touched her birthmark—just the lightest brush of a forefinger, but the contact shot something dark and electric through Tasha's body. The red stain tingled brilliantly, like newly uncorked champagne bubbling from the bottle.

"Do you feel your soul, lass? Here?"

She stared at him.

Understanding filled his gaze. "Aye, I thought so."

He stroked the birthmark again. A slow, deliberate stroke this time. The champagne mellowed, tingling and sparkling like stars. Heat sped through her veins; her pulse thundered in her ears. Her entire body hummed with restless elation.

A low, sensuous pull tugged at her belly. Kieran's grip on her arm tightened, urging her closer. His free hand cupped the back of her head. Her tongue darted between her lips; her gaze focused on the stubbled line of his jaw. With just the slightest movement, she could lean forward and taste him. The urge was almost overwhelming.

His eyes were twin shards of smoldering amber. His scent surrounded her, dark musk that weakened her knees. Her palm flattened on the hard plane of his chest, the coarse wool of his tartan rough under her touch. His heart pounded beneath her fingers, its beat every bit as wild as her own.

His gaze dropped to her lips; his sharp inhale was audible. *He's going to kiss me,* she thought in a daze. *And I'm going to let him...*

Footsteps. Angry. Behind her.

"Let her go, MacDonald. Now."

Kieran's head came up; his arms tightened around her like

bands of steel. Tasha wrenched her head around and gasped. Hunter stood on the path, not ten steps away. He held a tiny, silver-barreled pistol trained on Kieran's head.

Hunter advanced, gun unwavering. "Step away, MacDonald. You're far too big a target to miss, even with a woman as your shield."

"Ye wouldna shoot. Ye wouldna risk her."

"Would you?"

Kieran swore under his breath. Abruptly, he shoved Tasha to one side. The force sent her sprawling. Gravel bit into her knees; she swallowed a cry of pain. Hunter extended his arm, and for one awful second, Tasha was sure he was going to shoot.

"No!" she gasped. "Hunter, no! Are you crazy? He...he wasn't hurting me."

Hunter spared her a glance. "He had his hands on you."

"That's no reason to shoot him!"

"I think it is."

Kieran, incredibly, spread his arms. "Kill me then, man. Now. And put an end to this."

"No…" Tasha scrambled to her feet and grabbed Hunter's arm. "No. You can't."

Hunter frowned down at her. "The man's trespassing where he doesn't belong. He assaulted you. God only knows what he might have done if I hadn't stopped him."

"Nothing happened. I'm fine."

"He'll go to the constable, then," Hunter bit off. "I'll escort him there myself."

But when they turned, Kieran was gone.

"Thank God that scum didn't hurt you."

Hunter's tone held nothing but sheer relief, and his arm across Tasha's shoulder was nothing but comforting as they made their way back to the castle. Why, then, did it feel so...wrong?

"Who is he?"

"Vermin." Hunter spat the word. "A predator, and every man and woman in the village knows it. He should have been jailed last summer, after a village girl went missing. But nothing could be proven, and the blighter went free." He gave Tasha a long, measured look. "You had an extremely close call."

Extremely close. Just one second more and Kieran would have kissed her...

Hunter's jaw tightened. "It's a damn good thing I got there when I did."

Tasha looked up at him. "How did you find me? Just then, I mean?"

"You set off a silent alarm when you left the castle. I've been looking for you for over a half hour. It was foolish of you to go out alone, Tasha. Promise me you won't do it again."

She shook off his arm. "I'm not a child."

He exhaled. "I'm only trying to protect you."

He sounded so hurt that Tasha laid a hand on his arm and summoned a conciliatory smile. "I know. I had...I had no idea the garden wouldn't be safe."

"Come to me next time. I'm happy to escort you wherever you want to go."

They climbed the steps to the terrace, where a very pale Rossalyn stood wringing her hands. "Oh, my dear, you're all right. Whatever happened? Did you get lost?"

Grimly, Hunter recounted what had happened in the garden.

"That scoundrel!" Rossalyn exclaimed. "I'll see him locked up for this. Call the constable, Hunter."

"It's not necessary," Tasha insisted. "Really. All he did was talk to me."

"He tried to kiss you," Hunter said flatly.

The blood drained from Rossalyn's face, leaving her pale as a corpse. Her hand, claw-like, went to her throat.

"And did he?"

"No," Tasha hastened to assure her. "He didn't."

"Thank God," Rossalyn whispered.

"You should have shot him."

"In front of the girl, with her begging me not to? That hardly

would have helped our cause."

"MacDonald forces our hand. Now that he's touched her once, he'll soon return. We have to act quickly. You have to act quickly."

"It may be difficult. She's only known me a day, after all."

"MacDonald had her for mere minutes. Is he more a man than you?"

"No. Of course not."

"Then do what you must. Today." A pause. "She will understand, once it's over."

"Will you help me to my private parlor, Tasha?" Rossalyn asked halfway through the midday meal. "I don't feel very well, I'm afraid."

Tasha pushed her plate toward the center of the table. She didn't feel like eating, anyway. Her stomach was still churning from her early morning misadventure. Would Hunter really have killed Kieran? The very idea nauseated her.

Rossalyn leaned heavily on Tasha's arm as they ascended the stair to her suite of rooms.

"I am so sorry about what happened to you this morning," the older woman said. "I fear it was my fault, my dear. I should have known Kieran MacDonald would try to make trouble. He's cut from the same cloth as your father."

Tasha stopped in front of Rossalyn's door. "What do you mean by that?"

Rossalyn gave her a sad smile. "I don't mean to disillusion you, my dear, but your father—he was as deceitful as he was handsome. Glib, he was, and manipulative. Not a cent to his name. He lured my Maris into his web, thinking I would accept him as a son." She snorted. "As if a MacDonald could ever be fit for anything better than mucking out stables! He was after her inheritance, of course, but would she listen to me? No. She gave herself to the bounder. Then, when she became pregnant, I wouldn't allow her to ruin her life by marrying the scoundrel. That's when Ewan MacDonald realized Maris's fortune would not be lining his pockets. He abandoned her."

"I thought...I thought he was murdered."

"Murdered? Is that what Kieran MacDonald told you? It's

a lie. Ewan MacDonald died by his own folly. Stole a car, then ran it off a bridge in a heavy rain. I thought Maris would come to her senses, then, but she did not. She disappeared. And she was clever about it. I hired the best investigators, but it was years before they located her."

Tasha was silent as she tried to reconcile her grandmother's description of her father with the glowing picture Kieran had painted of him. She couldn't. Who was lying?

She opened the door to Rossalyn's room. "But...all that happened so long ago. It has nothing to do with Kieran MacDonald. He was a young boy when all that happened."

"He's a MacDonald. Blood will tell, Tasha."

I'm a MacDonald, too, she wanted to shout. Instead, she said, "I just don't see why Hunter felt he had to threaten the poor man with a gun."

"Don't you? MacDonald tried to kiss you! It's natural enough for a man like Hunter to defend his woman from an interloper."

"But...I'm not Hunter's woman."

"You will be. He's quite taken with you, you know."

Tasha stared. "He only met me yesterday."

Rossalyn smiled. "It's called love at first sight. You have my blessing, of course. Hunter is a fine man." She gave Tasha a little push, propelling her across the threshold and into the parlor. "I'm an incorrigible romantic, you know. I do hope you'll forgive this little trick. All the better to encourage you, my dear."

Before Tasha could reply, she found the door shut gently but firmly in her face. A key scraped. Tasha gaped at the knob for one long moment before she grasped it and twisted, to no avail.

Rossalyn had locked her in.

A floorboard creaked. She spun around to find Hunter standing in the center of the room, watching her. He'd removed his jacket; it was folded neatly over the back of a chair. The glint of possession in his eyes sent a shiver down her spine.

"Hunter. What's going on?"

Hunter moved toward her. Her birthmark burned. Tasha shrank back, her spine pressing against the door.

"It's simple, really," he said. "You're to become my lover."

"You're insane. I don't sleep with men I barely know!"

"No? You were about to spread your legs for MacDonald."

Tasha gasped her outrage. "I certainly was n…"

Hunter's hands closed on her shoulders. His eyes were heavy-lidded, his smile seductive. A chill sank into her bones.

His thumb traced the line of her collarbone. "I advise you not to fight me, Tasha. You won't win. Our joining is inevitable. Here. I'll show you." He drew back, slipping the cufflink from his left shirt sleeve. Rolling up the sleeve, he presented his wrist for her inspection.

She stared at the red mark. "You…you have the same birthmark I do?"

He nodded. "As does Rossalyn. But since her birth, no other females of our clan have been born marked. Until you. Do you know what that means?"

Tasha shook her head.

"It means, my Tasha, that you are mine."

He pressed her up against the door and covered her mouth with his. Tasha nearly gagged. Twisting, she managed to jab an elbow into his gut.

Hunter barked a sharp curse. With efficient movements, he wrapped his arms around her and hauled her across the room. She caught a glimpse of his destination—a sofa—and launched into a frenzy of kicks and punches.

He laughed as he threw her down on the couch, easily capturing her flailing limbs. Pinning her wrists over her head, he ran a proprietary hand over her body.

"Stop it, Tasha. You'll only hurt yourself. You can't change what's going to happen. We're fated to be together. The birthmarks prove it."

"You're insane. How could you do this?"

"Don't you understand yet? You're the clan's only marked female of childbearing age. One of our marked males has to have you, or the gift will pass from the MacLeods forever. Rossalyn has decided that you will be mine." He paused. "At the very least, you will not be *his*."

"You're talking about Kieran."

He bared his teeth. "I should have killed the bastard when I had the chance."

"Kieran...does he have the mark, too?"

"He does. Little good it will do him after you're mine. The MacDonalds have no marked females."

"Except me," Tasha said.

Hunter's eyes glinted dangerously. He grabbed the hem of her tee shirt and ripped the garment over her head, taking her bra with it. He twisted the fabric around her wrists, binding them.

"You," he said. "Are mine."

Panic slid though her. "No. Please. Don't do this…"

"No more talking."

He unsnapped her waistband of her jeans and yanked at the zipper. Tasha writhed and bucked, but her struggles only seemed to encourage him. He yanked off her jeans and panties.

Her breath came in spurts. *God, no.* This could not be happening.

He started working his belt.

Help. Please.

In the deepest recesses of her mind, an answer came. *I am coming.* An instant later, a large, canine shadow passed by the window.

Tasha's birthmark tingled. A revelation struck. She went absolutely still. The mark. The gift. The wolf.

Her dazed mind refused to absorb the possibility. It was insane.

Wasn't it?

Hunter, alerted by the sudden cessation of Tasha's struggles, looked down. She stared back, every muscle rigid, her heart thudding against her ribs.

"You...you're... Kieran, too, he's... Oh, my *God*."

The window above the sofa exploded, showering broken glass and splintered wood down on the sofa. A snarling blur hurtled overhead.

The massive black wolf landed and turned in one smooth,

savage movement.

Hunter let out an unholy growl. Tasha's eyes went wide as he leaped backward, his clothes ripping to shreds as a dark light rippled over his body. Tasha scuttled upright, tearing at the shirt binding her wrists as Hunter, the man, changed into a snarling wolf.

The two beasts, one black, one gray, circled the small room, heads lowered, teeth bared, fur bristling along their spines. Then, in a blur of movement, they sprang.

The fight was short and brutal. At the end, the gray wolf lay belly up, its enemy's teeth at its throat. The black wolf gave its victim a shake, then, in a magnanimous show of mercy, raised its head. Whimpering, the gray wolf scrambled under a table, tail tucked between its legs.

The black wolf looked at Tasha.

"Did I come in time, lass?"

She wasn't insane. She *wasn't*. She'd heard his voice in her mind.

"K...Kieran? Are you...are you the wolf?"

"Aye. 'Tis I, lass." His golden eyes pinned her in place. *"Did I come in time?"* he repeated, his gaze sweeping down her body.

Tasha abruptly realized she was naked. "Y...yes. Yes, you did." She glanced at the gray wolf that was Hunter, cowering under a table. "He didn't hurt me."

Deep emotion shuddered through his massive, furred body. *"Taing do Dhia."* Thank God.

"How did you know I needed you?"

"I heard your call."

"In...in your mind? Like I'm hearing you now?"

"Aye. Mates can communicate this way, as long as one of them has the form of a wolf."

She had trouble catching her breath. *"One* of us? What does that mean, exactly?"

His golden wolf's eyes caressed her. *"You and I bear the mark of the moon. You have the gift, as I do. And...I would have you as my mate.* His regal head lowered in respect. *If you will accept me."*

Tasha looked into Kieran's amber eyes, and something deep in her soul clicked into place.

"Will you have me, m'leannán? Will you be my mate?"

Her heart trembled. Her birthmark tingled in soaring, expanding joy.

"Yes. Yes, Kieran. I'll have you."

And she began to change.

Two black wolves loped out of the castle and dashed through the deepening shadows. A moment later, a gray wolf staggered through the door and onto the terrace, blood dripping from a nasty gash on its flank.

A silver she-wolf stepped from the shadows.

The gray wolf lowered its head and tucked its tail between its legs.

The she-wolf's gaze fixed on the cavorting blacks. She had intervened between lovers once before, when her daughter had turned her back on the pack, but now? She was soul-tired. Defeated. If the powerful male she'd raised from a pup could not triumph, there was naught she could do but accept her defeat.

Standing still as a statue, Rossalyn MacLeod watched her granddaughter and her chosen mate melt into the forest gloaming.

The End

Joy Nash is the *USA Today* bestselling author of *Immortals: The Awakening, Immortals: The Crossing,* and the *Druids of Avalon* historical fantasy series. Check out Joy's new paranormal series *Watchers* at www.joynash.com.

Midnight on the Double-B

Kayce Lassiter

In a cloud of dust, Kylah McCombs' truck skidded to a stop in front of the sprawling ranch house on the Double-B. She was out of the truck and half way to the front steps when the door opened and a tall, lean man stepped onto the porch. The straw-colored cowboy hat shaded his face, so Kylah wasn't sure which of the Beasty boys he was.

"I want to speak to that low-bellied snake, Michael Beasty. Is he here?" Kylah was in no mood to mince words. That monster would get a piece of her mind.

"I'm Michael Beasty." He tipped his head to the side and his eyes narrowed as the sunlight reached beneath his hat. "What can I do for you, Miss…?"

Kylah almost missed a step. This gorgeous man with the steel-gray eyes and sandy hair curling just above his collar was Michael Beasty? He'd come a long way from the skinny, gangly kid she remembered. With a deep breath, she stopped about ten feet from the porch steps and threw her shoulders back. "McCombs…Kylah McCombs. Ring a bell? It should. You just stole my land, you low-down…"

"Ah, Miss McCombs," he interrupted, not moving from the high ground of the porch. "I expected your father to come by. He send you to do his dirty work?"

Kylah took control of her anger as his barb wrapped around her heart and squeezed. He was baiting her and he would not win.

"My father did not send me. I came to see for myself what kind of snake takes advantage of an old man."

The muscles in his jaw ground as he leaned against a post

and crossed his arms.

What an arrogant bastard! The hairs on the back of her neck stood up.

"Maybe your old man should've paid his taxes."

"You stole that land and you know it!"

"I bought it fair and square."

Kylah's head pounded as the blood rushed at her temples. "I'll buy it back. I'll pay you exactly what you paid for it."

He laughed. "It's not for sale."

"With men like you, everything is for sale. What's your price?" She'd stepped into a bucket of crap and given up bargaining position. Now she'd pay big time for her father's mistake. Well, there was no money. Kylah had bluffed, stalling for time and hoping something would fall into place for her...just one break.

Michael Beasty stared hard, as if he saw a price written on her forehead.

"Triple."

"What?!" Kylah shrieked as panic shot through her. She'd expected the man to be a beast, but this was outrageous. He'd stolen the land with the only irrigation source for her ranch, and for pennies on the dollar. Everyone in the county knew the land belonged to the McCombs family and had always respected that. Until now. Michael Beasty clearly intended to drive them out of business. But why?

Michael said nothing as he stared at her through cold gray eyes.

Kylah swallowed the lump in her throat as she grasped for rational thought. "That will ruin us and you know it," she whispered. She hated the pleading edge to her voice, but the panic sat like a heavy rock in the pit of her stomach as the roaring in her ears threatened to consume her mind.

"What the hell?" Michael Beasty stared over her head, toward the road.

She turned and realized the roaring in her ears was the sound of a motorcycle approaching ahead of a huge cloud of dust. Thankful for the distraction, she used the next few seconds to regroup, determined not to be derailed.

Old Man Beasty had passed away last year and his oldest son had returned to run the ranch. She'd expected to be able to raise a fuss and have the man offer a solution. His father had been a fair man—honest and reasonable. Something his son clearly was not. Now she was in a battle for her ranch, a battle for her life.

Kylah turned away from the dust cloud that rolled over her as the huge Harley came to a stop just a few feet away.

"Well crap!" A woman's disembodied voice came from the center of the cloud of dust, followed by coughing. "Damn," the woman muttered between coughs. "I sure didn't expect that. The freakin' handbook didn't say anything about dust. I'll have to have another talk with that damn, cocky Godfather."

Kylah turned toward the motorcycle and found the most bizarre sight. The rider was a woman who looked like a reject from *Cowboys and Indians* magazine. She appeared to be about sixty years old, wearing dark red Wranglers and cowboy boots, a cherry colored tank top, and a bright red cowboy hat perched on top of a full head of long curly red hair. At about five foot six, she couldn't have been a hundred pounds dripping wet.

She wasn't from around here.

Kylah heard Michael mutter, "What the hell is that?"

There was no answer for his question.

"Well, you two just gonna stand there gawkin' at me or ya gonna offer a lady a drink?" The woman in red dropped the kickstand, dismounted and did a slow swagger toward them like she owned the joint.

Kylah looked over her shoulder to find Michael descending the steps, blinking like a mole in sunlight. He opened his mouth as his right boot hit the dirt, but nothing came out. He stopped at the base of the steps.

The woman threw back her head and laughed a hearty, throaty laugh. Then her brown eyes focused on Michael. "Now, what kind of fight is this? I expected to find you two with your hands wrapped around each other's throats, rolling around in the dirt—or maybe at least one gun drawn. How disappointing."

Michael stood speechless for a few seconds, but he still found his voice before Kylah. "Fight? What are you talking about? And while we're at it, who the hell are you? What do you want?" He didn't wait for an answer, but stared at Kylah and asked, "She with you?"

Kylah shook her head. Her long, silky strawberry-blond hair bouncing softly on her shoulders made his gut clench. The woman was certainly beautiful. She had huge, expressive green eyes with long, thick lashes you could almost count and a sprinkling of freckles over the bridge of her nose. Michael stared longer than he should have. He hadn't seen her in over a decade, but the years since high school had been kind to her. Very kind. She was probably five foot seven or eight and put together like a Greek goddess in Wranglers and boots—just the kind of woman to confuse a man into giving up his water rights. Probably why her father sent her.

Michael cleared his throat and returned his attention to the crazy old broad who'd ridden in on the motorcycle.

"My name's Delta Jane and as for what I want…well, right now I want a drink. I'm gonna have a lot of work to do in about two switches of a cow's tail." With a wave of her hand, she sauntered past Michael and started up the steps to his house.

"Excuse me," Michael called as he followed her to the porch, but before he could even reach the steps, the front door flew open and his housekeeper barreled through with a suitcase in each hand, issuing a string of Spanish curse words at him that almost made his ears blister.

Delta Jane dodged the woman with the suitcases and slipped inside just before the screen door slammed shut.

"Hortense, what the hell are you doin'?" Michael demanded. "Where you goin'?"

She glared at Michael as she passed him, punctuating her curses with shakes of her head as she lugged her suitcases to an old red primered pickup truck and threw them in the back. She hopped in the cab and cranked the engine over before scolding him in broken English through the truck's open window.

"I no mind cook for you and your brothers. But I no like cook for all cowboys. You say, 'Stay, Hortense, I pay you more.' Now you bring home big hairy dog. He eat my biscuits, pee on my dress. I not feed ugly dog. You not pay me enough. I go."

"What? What dog?" Michael lunged to stop the truck, but was too late.

Hortense peeled out, spraying gravel in her wake, as he tucked his head under his arm to avoid being pelted in the face with flying gravel.

"Damn!" He stared after the old truck, hoping to see brake lights. Now what? He had a dozen hungry cowboys to feed. Without a housekeeper, he'd be cooking the meals himself. How would he keep up with his work? Hell, half the ranch hands would probably quit inside the first week.

It had taken him three months to find someone who would work at the wages he could afford. Now she was gone. He had no cook and, thanks to the McCombs family, he also had no money.

Which reminded him, he had an emergency of another kind brewing—a beautiful, sharp-tongued woman, who'd apparently been sent by her father to make him forget all about the land he'd just spent his last dollar on in order to save his ranch.

When Michael headed back toward the house, he found Kylah McCombs staring at him.

"Wow, that was dramatic. What'd you do to her?"

Michael stopped in front of her and growled, "You still here?" Without waiting for an answer, he continued. "Why don't you just take yourself on home and tell daddy you failed. He'll have to find another way to con me out of that land."

"Con you out of..." Kayla's face flushed and she took a step forward with her fists clenched. For a second, Michael thought she'd take a swing at him. Just as he started to take a step back, the front door slammed open again and the strange old broad who had ridden in on the motorcycle came strutting out and dropped onto the bench to the left of the front door.

"Woo hoo, now it's gettin' exciting."

"You still here too?" Michael demanded.

"Yep. Got work to do."

"I don't suppose you..." Before Michael could ask the woman if she cooked, a huge gray dog nosed open the front door and padded onto the porch. He sidled over to the woman in red. She scratched him behind the ear and he clumsily dropped to the floor and curled up at her feet.

"Cute, ain't he?" the woman asked of no one in particular. "But he needs a good bath and a brush."

Michael stared at the dog with its long, gray matted fur and feet that looked like enormous dust mops dipped in mud. Strings of dreadlocks hung from the bottom of its belly, long enough to drag the ground when the dog was standing. There were no visible signs of eyes anywhere on the animal, but Michael assumed they must be somewhere near the short, floppy ears hanging off the end pointed toward him. Where'd the dog come from? Did he belong to the dingbat on the motorcycle?

Michael started back toward the porch. "That your dog?" He asked, pointing to the filthy gray fleabag at the woman's feet and wondering if it smelled as bad as it looked.

"Nope, he's your dog now."

"My dog!" Michael stopped in his tracks about two feet from the bottom step of the porch. "Whoa. Lady, I don't own a dog and I don't want one." With a hard look at the pile of matted fur, he added, "And if I did own a dog, I wouldn't own one as ugly as that."

Delta Jane looked down and patted the dog on the head. "Don't take it personally, Brutus, he doesn't mean it."

Michael looked at the woman suspiciously. "Lady, if you think you're going to foist that flea-bitten piece of canine carcass on me, you're crazy as a loon. You got a name for him, he's your dog. Now, take your dog and get off my property."

Delta narrowed her eyes and fixed her glare on Michael as she scooted the dog out of the way with one red boot and rose. He heard the clock ticking on the living room wall inside the house as she moved to the edge of the porch and descended the front steps.

At the foot of the steps, she stopped and pointed one long, red lacquered nail at him. "You keep a civil tongue in your head, young man, or I'll see to it you're scratching flea bites for a year."

"What?" Who the hell was this crazy woman, where did that damn dog come from, and what the hell were all these people doing in his front yard? Michael's head pounded like there was a ten pound sledge hammer trying to break through his skull.

She continued to point that long red nail at him. "You need a cook." She stopped a moment for effect, her finger moving closer to Michael's face. "You have no money to pay for one, but you have something she wants."

The nail moved to point at Kylah like the needle of a compass. "She can cook." Another pause for effect. "She has no money to pay for the land she wants back, but she's a damn good cook."

Michael was too confused to move. All he could do was watch the woman in red as she turned away, strutted to the Harley, mounted, and smiled at them.

"You two do the math. I'll be around if you need me."

Delta turned the key she'd left hanging in the ignition. Then reached down with her left hand and flipped the toggle on the gas, pushed the starter button, and cranked the gas with her right hand. The Harley roared to life as smoke shot out the back of pipes that looked like a sawed off shotgun. Kicking it into gear, the woman made a wide turn in the driveway and sprayed a rooster tail of gravel fifteen feet in the air as she fishtailed down the drive.

Kylah was the first to break the silence this time. "Holy crap! You got some strange friends."

"Me? I thought she was with you."

"Nope, never saw her before and she sure was comfortable in your house and with your dog."

"Well, she's not my friend. I never saw her before either…and that's not my damn dog!"

Kylah's eyes shifted left. She smiled as she focused on the

area in front of the bench by the door.

Michael followed her gaze and there on his front porch, snoring, was the incredible ugly hulk. Michael groaned and scrubbed at his face with his hands. "God, could this day get any worse?"

Then it dawned on him. The old broad had offered a solution to his problems. Kylah could cook. Maybe he could stand her sharp tongue long enough to find another cook. If he paid her in credit against repurchase of the land, it would give him time to sort out what to do about the land he'd acquired. The McCombs family had always owned that strip of land the river flowed on, but he'd be damned if he'd risk losing access to the only irrigation source for his ranch just because the old man wouldn't pay his taxes. Maybe the gal on the Harley had something, after all.

Michael looked at Kylah and his breath hitched. The sun glinted off her hair like burning red gold. Those incredible eyes got him in the gut as she watched him. He wondered for a second if he could even manage to hold onto that land long enough to find another cook? Or would this woman end up walking away with the title in her back pocket within the first twenty four hours? Damn, she took his breath away.

"Can you really cook?" His throat was dry and his voice raspy.

"What? Are you suggesting I go to work for you? Of course I can cook, but I have my own ranch to run. Why would I want to come to work for you, anyway?"

"You want your land back. I hold the title. I could pay you the same wages I was paying Hortense and credit your salary against the cost of the land."

Kylah appeared to think it over for a moment. Then she shook her head. "You tripled the cost over what you paid for the back taxes. And you probably underpaid that poor housekeeper. Not a good deal."

He flinched as she cut him to the bone. She was right, but he couldn't afford to pay more. He needed time. "Okay, I'll reduce the price to double what I paid."

Kylah rolled her eyes. "Oh, Mr. Generous." She chewed

on her lower lip…a very pink, very luscious lip. "You'd have to pay me twice what you were paying her."

"Twice? Are you nuts? I'll go twelve dollars an hour. That's a helluvalot more than Hortense was making and more than most ranch cooks make."

"Deal."

Her quick response rocked him back on his heels. Damn! He'd offered too much. Well, it was too late now.

"Okay. You can move your stuff in today. I need you to start with dinner tonight."

"Move my stuff in?"

"Yeah. Three meals a day, laundry for a dozen ranch hands, and cleaning the main house. I need someone here on-site. You can have Sundays off and as long as the chores are done, you come and go as you please in the evenings."

Michael didn't draw a breath as he waited for her answer. Why did it matter so much to him?

"All right. But I can't start until tomorrow. I'll have to make arrangements to have my niece fill in for me. We got folks to feed over there too."

When he opened his mouth to protest, she held up a hand. "Remember, Mr. Beasty, I also have a ranch to run. I'll find a way to sell myself into indentured servitude to the devil to save it, but it will take me another day."

He shut his mouth and nodded, relief flooding through him. She'd be back.

As she turned to go, she added, "I'll see you tomorrow about one."

Michael had no idea why it mattered so much that she'd return, but it did.

As he entered the house, the screen door banged shut behind him. He heard the engine in her truck start and the groan of the transmission as she put it in gear. Like a man under a spell, he turned back to lean against the inside of the door frame and watch her speed down his driveway.

Kylah. The most beautiful, frustrating woman he'd ever met…and she'd be back tomorrow to move into his house. Could he keep her out of his heart? Did he even want to?

From her vantage point high on a hill overlooking the Double-B Ranch, a woman watched the scene play out between Kylah and Michael. Her supernatural hearing allowed her to catch every word that passed between the two.

Muttering to herself, she waved her right hand in the air as if swinging a lariat over her head. When she cast the imaginary rope in the direction of the farm house, sparks flew from the tips of her fingers.

She smiled as the sparkle of her spell settled over the house and the two arguing in the front yard. Lifting the red cowboy hat from the handlebar where it hung, she snugged it on her head and settled herself on the seat.

"Now, let's see just how long it takes you to realize you're truly caught, Mr. Beasty."

Bone tired, Michael closed the gate and headed for the house. It was two o'clock and he hoped Kylah McCombs had kept her word. Twenty-four hours of pulling double duty had him dead on his feet.

The blue Ford truck parked in front of the house indicated she must be here. He started at the warm, fuzzy feeling spreading through his gut. Okay, so it would be nice to have a pretty woman around. That's all it was, just the sight of a pretty woman, sort of like a vase of flowers on the table. Nothing more. But the triple-beat of his heart told a different story.

He wiped his boots as he entered to the incredible smells of pies baking in the oven. Hortense never baked and most of her meals were thrown together from cans. He sniffed. Cinnamon and apples. The smell made his mouth water.

Just inside the kitchen door, he froze. The feeling that he'd just stepped into a Norman Rockwell picture settled over him like a warm coat in a winter freeze—the sun streaming in through the window, pots steaming on the stove, and the table set for dinner. Kylah stood at the sink with her back to him, humming a popular country song and swaying from side to side as she peeled potatoes. The picture she presented, with her red-gold hair streaming down her back, the characteristic "W" of Wrangler jeans peeking through the split in her apron, showed just enough to make him want to see more.

Kylah turned to drop the peeled potato into a bowl. With a yelp, she jumped and threw the potato. He caught it just before it clubbed him in the forehead.

"Something I said?" he asked with the most insolent grin he could muster. Jerking her chain could be fun.

"Oh my God, you scared the devil out of me!"

"I doubt that."

She scowled. "Sneak up on me like that again and it might be a knife in my hand next time. Then I'd have to explain blood on the biscuits."

Michael still wondered if she really knew how to throw a knife when she hurled an oven mitt at him. "Here. Make yourself useful. There's pies in the oven and they should be ready to come out right about now."

She had pluck. He'd give her that.

He pulled the first pie from the oven and set it on the stovetop, inhaling deeply. "Mmmmm…apple. Mmm…my favorite."

"Humph, then I'll make sure I don't make that mistake again."

A quick peek from the corner of his eye showed a slight up-turn at the corner of her mouth. She wasn't serious. He'd get apple pie again.

Three more pies came out of the oven—another apple and two cherries. Yum! A huge pot of stew bubbled on the stove next to a pot of water for the potatoes. "You do all this in an hour?"

Kylah dropped the last peeled potato onto the pile. "No. My niece and I worked all night fixing re-heatable meals for the boys over at my place. I doubled the amounts and brought half of it over here. You owe me for the cost of supplies…" With a hard look, she added, "That part will be cash."

He smiled. "No problem, just write up a detailed receipt and I'll cut you a check on Friday. We generally do the ranch shopping on Mondays. I'll drive you into town so you've got help with the bags and such."

She efficiently diced potatoes and dropped them into the boiling water, saying nothing until he turned to leave the kitchen.

"Dinner will be ready at six and I expect the boys to be cleaned up before they come to the table. If they're late, the biscuits will be cold."

He grinned, but didn't turn. She might not like him, but she held her own. He liked her spunk.

"I'll tell 'em."

At the doorway, he stopped and turned to focus on something that just now registered. The dog. That big, ugly, dirty dog had disappeared last night right after Kylah left. But it was now sprawled on the kitchen floor like a hog in the sun.

"What's up with your dog? Can't you leave him at home?"

"I told you, he's not my dog. He followed me home last night and refused to leave. He was sitting on my porch when I left this morning and standing on your porch when I pulled in. How he beat me here, I have no idea. He's your dog…you tell me."

"He's not my dog. I wouldn't have a dog that ugly." Michael shook his head as he stomped out of the kitchen. Two could play that game. If she didn't want to admit it was her dog, he didn't give a damn.

Kylah took a deep breath when she heard the front door thump shut. The man made her nervous as a long-tailed cat in a room full of rocking chairs and she was happy to have him out of her kitchen. Well, it was his kitchen, technically. But as long as she worked here, it was hers. It wouldn't be easy running two households, especially with a man she hated underfoot. If only he weren't so damn good looking. It was a real distraction. But then, that was the way with evil. It often came in pretty packages.

A loud pop startled Kylah and she spun around to find the woman who had ridden in on the Harley the day before standing in front of the stove, fingering one of the pies.

"Oooh, these smell good. I'll just have a piece of this apple pie before it cools."

Kylah raised her wooden spoon like a weapon and stepped toward her. "You keep your hands off that pie. It's for the boys for dinner and I won't have you cutting into it now."

Delta rolled her bright green eyes at the raised spoon. "Okay, okay, don't have a cow. I won't touch your precious pie."

Kylah stared at the woman, dressed from head to toe in lime green. Even her hair was a greenish-blonde. "I would have sworn you had brown eyes and red hair."

Delta turned and leaned back against the counter next to the stove, her arms crossed over her chest. "You ever hear of hair dye and contacts?"

"I've never seen hair dye quite that color, except maybe at Halloween."

"Don't be a smart ass, girlie. You have to special order this stuff and the guy I get it from has a bit of an attitude today. So don't press your luck."

Delta pushed away from the counter and turned back to the stove. When she lifted the lid to the stew pot sitting on the back burner and sniffed, Kylah noticed the tattoo on her shoulder for the first time that read, "Bite Me, Cowboy."

"Nice," Kylah muttered to herself as she went to the refrigerator.

"You like it?"

"Like what?"

"The tattoo. You like it?"

Kylah struggled for a moment with a smart-ass retort. "It's...well, it's unique. Suits you." Delta really didn't seem all that bad, just a bit weird.

"Thanks. I like unique. That'll work."

"How'd you get here anyway? I didn't hear your motorcycle pull in."

"Ah, I didn't feel like eating dust today, so I just popped in."

Kylah smiled to herself. "On your broom?"

After a moment of silence, she turned to find the strange woman looking at her with a self-satisfied grin. "Honey, it don't make no sense for you to go pissin' off your Fairy Godmother at a time like this. You're gonna need me to get out of this jam and catch that handsome young beast you're working for."

Oh my God, she's crazy.

"Nope," the woman replied, "not crazy."

Kylah stared at her. "Did I say that out loud?"

"No."

"You psychic?"

"You might say that, but your thoughts are the only ones I can hear."

Oh, my freaking luck. If she really were my Fairy Godmother, I'd have to shoot myself. Now how do I get this crazy bitch out of my kitchen?

"Oh, now that's just downright rude."

"What? What's rude?" Kylah's heart pounded in her chest. This was getting creepy.

"Calling me a crazy bitch just isn't right. I'm standing right here. I'm a terrific Fairy Godmother. You're just lucky it's me and not that hair-brained Gretta, always parading around in a thong bikini she shouldn't be caught dead in. Tough to find a place to look when you're talking to that one."

Kylah stared. *What the hell?*

"Now, let's talk about that handsome Michael Beasty."

"Let's not."

The woman pointed a sharp, green nail at Kylah. "You're as rude as your young man. Keep it up and I'll file to get you another FGM. I don't have to do this, you know."

"Do what exactly?"

"Get you married off to that handsome man you're working for."

"What?" Kylah's voice jumped about three octaves. "Married? To the devil?"

Delta Jane's eyebrows rose sharply. "To the devil? Nooooo. That would be a special assignment, requiring an FGM from the Special Forces Unit. I'm only regional."

Kylah's brain shut down the second the old woman mentioned marriage to Michael Beasty. And to make matters worse, every cell in her body applauded the concept.

What the hell?

"Delta, I don't know what Michael's game is…or yours…but I didn't just fall off the turnip truck. He stole that strip of land with the river on it, but he's not getting my whole ranch. So don't let the door hit you in the butt on your way out."

Delta groaned and rolled her eyes to the ceiling. "Why me? Why do I always get the stubborn ones with fresh mouths?" She paused and cocked her head as if listening to a voice from the ceiling. "Oh, very funny. Yeah? Well, you can just kiss my ass!"

Kylah watched Delta's bizarre behavior. The woman was clearly unbalanced, but Kylah couldn't resist looking up to make sure there wasn't someone, or something, hovering up in the corner of the kitchen.

"What? Mark the spot?" Delta continued her rant. "I'll show you 'mark the spot', you smart aleck." With that, Delta undid her belt and zipper and dropped the back of her pants to bare one cheek. "There, kiss that!"

Kylah couldn't believe it. Delta Jane was bent over in the middle of her kitchen with her pants dropped and high on her right butt cheek was another tattoo—a set of red lips.

"What the hell is going on in here?"

Michael's voice boomed from the doorway, causing Kylah to jump.

"Holy Mother of God, you scared me to death!" Kylah drew a deep breath and covered her chest with her hand while Delta casually zipped and buckled her pants.

"Nothing," was Delta's only reply as she shot a murderous look at the spot on the ceiling. Without another word, she breezed past Michael toward the front room.

He looked at Kylah and asked, "What was that?"

She shrugged. "I don't know." Then, staring after Delta, she asked, "Did you know she has a pair of lips tattooed on her butt?"

Michael closed his eyes. *Do I really need a cook this bad?* "I don't give a rip what she's got tattooed where. Just have your friend keep her pants on."

"My friend? You're the one who sent her in here to convince me to marry you!"

Michael felt like he'd been poleaxed. "What? Marry? Why the hell would I want to marry you? You're as crazy as she is!"

As he watched the hurt flit across Kylah's eyes, the bottom dropped out of Michael's stomach. What was she talking about? He turned to stare after Delta Jane. What was the old woman's game? Maybe he should just fire Kylah and be done with it. Maybe then he'd be rid of this woman and her bizarre sidekick, not to mention the big, ugly dog.

But when he opened his mouth to do it, nothing came out. He stared into the deep pools of Kylah's huge green eyes and just couldn't utter the words. He couldn't fire her. The land belonged to her and he knew it. He might have paid the back taxes to gain temporary control, but he wasn't the kind of man who could permanently strip her of ownership. Both ranches needed that piece of land to survive and as Michael stared into Kylah's eyes, he knew deep in his gut he would find a way to save both ranches, even if it killed him—and it just might if these two women had any say in it.

Dinner on a working ranch was always a simple affair—plenty of food, dusty boots, clean hands, and good natured banter. So despite the fact she didn't know this crew, Kylah had no qualms about fitting in. Cowboys were cowboys and she'd grown up with men just like the ones now filing through the door to sit at her table.

Dinner went quickly, with the cowboys making their way through the bowls and platters of food like a plague of locusts. There was lots of lighthearted teasing around the table and even a round of applause when Kylah brought the pies out to the table.

After dinner, the boys all headed out to settle into the bunkhouse while Kylah washed up the dinner dishes. She started when Michael returned from the living room and began to dry the dishes and put them away.

He caught her looking at him from the corner of her eye

and asked, "What?"

"Nothing. I'm just surprised at you drying dishes."

Sidling up next to her, he playfully bumped her with his hip as he dried a plate. "You don't think I can dry dishes or you think I think it's woman's work?"

Grudgingly, her opinion of him rose a notch. "Just didn't expect it, is all."

He pinned her with a penetrating look. "This isn't a country club. If my people are working, I'm working."

Kylah sensed something jump between them, like invisible sparks, as she stared into his eyes. Uncomfortable, she turned away. But her eyes returned to stare at his back when he reached to slide a platter onto the top shelf. He really was an amazingly handsome man, tall and lean. As her gaze traveled downward, she noticed his narrow hips. Hard work had definitely fine tuned that incredible body. With a flush, she tore her eyes away. How could a man like that have such a hard heart?

The close proximity to Michael grated on Kylah, so she hurried through the dishes, anxious to be outside where she could catch her breath. She didn't know what it was about the man, but when he stood so close to her at the counter she could feel the heat from his body. It seemed the oxygen was being sucked from the room.

"That's it," she announced as she pulled the plug in the sink. Wiping her hands on her apron, she reached back to untie it, only to find Michael had beaten her to it. When her hands met his, she inhaled sharply and jerked her hands forward as her stomach did a loop-de-loop.

Michael stepped away. "Sorry. Uh...goodnight." He was at the door to the living room in three steps, where he stopped but didn't turn around. "Thanks. Dinner was good." He cleared his throat, but said nothing more as he left her alone in the kitchen.

Kylah's heart pounded like she'd just run a marathon. Frustrated at her inability to control her reaction to Michael Beasty, she muttered to herself, "Stupid girl. What the hell's the matter with you? That man is the enemy. Get over it!"

She flung her apron over the back of a chair and headed out the back door. A walk under the stars was just what she needed to clear her brain.

Unfamiliar with the ranch, Kylah wandered out past the barn and down a well-worn path. Following it to the end, she found herself at the edge of a small watering hole where she sat on a grassy spot at the edge of the trees. It was a cool night and the branches of the trees rustled as a light breeze fluttered through. She inhaled the clean, fresh smell of running water, mixed with the smell of grass and pine needles.

Staring at the water, her mind drifted as she watched the moonlight play across its surface. Within minutes, it occurred to her this pond must be fed by a waterway branching off of the same river that ran through her property—or, rather, the property Michael Beasty had stolen from her. The bile rose in her throat. If he could gain control of the valley's only water source, Michael stood to make a mint off of selling water to the neighboring ranch. Or, worse yet, he could bankrupt her family and force them out. With that done, he would be in a perfect position to buy the land for a song.

Suddenly, she was exhausted. It had been an emotional day and now she had to admit she was hopelessly infatuated with a man who had the power to ruin everything her father had spent a lifetime building. She lay down on her side and pulled her knees to her chest, feeling very alone and lost.

Kylah woke with a start, disoriented. *Where am I?* Her heart pounded as the blood rushed in her ears, but it was something else that woke her. There—the snap of a twig. She wasn't alone.

Kylah inhaled quietly and raised up on one elbow to look around. Michael Beasty emerged from the trees, head down and apparently absorbed in thought. She didn't move fast enough to get out of his way.

He spotted her a split second before he fell over her. Crashing to the ground on top of her, Michael instinctively pulled Kylah to him as he rolled to avoid crushing her. A sharp elbow to the ribs knocked the wind out of him. He couldn't be sure, but he had a good idea she'd intended the elbow hit.

Sucking air into his lungs, he scrambled to protect other body parts as the woman foundered around, poking and kicking, in an effort to stand.

"Dammit, woman, stop before you hurt someone!"

Michael managed to capture both her hands in his and pull her into a sitting position as he rolled to his knees, only to find himself nose to nose with the beauty. Her eyes widened, with the look of a wild deer and suddenly the elbow to the stomach didn't compare to the invisible band constricting itself around his heart.

He released her hands and sat back on his heels as she scooted away from him.

"Sorry. I didn't mean to startle you." With a moan, he rubbed his stomach and added, "Or fall on you."

"Humph," was Kylah's only reply.

But she didn't move to leave, so Michael swung around and sat next to her, his long legs stretched out in front of him. Neither spoke as they quietly looked out over the water.

Michael broke the silence. "I come here a lot at night to think. You like it?"

"Yeah, I do. Where did the ranch get its name?"

"My great-grandfather won the land in a poker game. His name was Buford Beasty, so the ranch became the Double-B."

She nodded. "Is it spring-fed?"

"What?"

"The pond. Is it spring-fed?"

This was dangerous territory. Any discussion of where the water in this pond came from would lead to the land they fought over.

"No." Michael's mind raced to find a different subject. "What kind of name is Kylah? I don't think I've ever heard it before."

In the moonlight, he saw her eyes search his face as if she were looking for some motivation behind the question. "Irish. My ancestors are Irish."

He nodded. "What does it mean?"

Michael would have sworn the question embarrassed her. Even in the dimmed light of the moon, he thought he saw her cheeks darken. When she didn't answer, he tried again.

"It's an unusual name. Must mean something."

"Beauty. It's Gaelic. The original spelling was C-a-d-h-l-a, but it's pronounced KY-lah. My folks went with the phonetic spelling, hoping to make life easier." Profound silence fell for the span of a few heartbeats before she added, "When I was little, my mom used to tell me it implied a beauty only poets can describe. Silly, huh? But to a little girl, it was the stuff of fairy tales."

How fitting. As if the name had evoked some sort of spell, Michael found himself entranced by the sight of the woman with the light from the full moon casting shadows across her face. He couldn't look away. Reaching out, he took her hand in his. "It's not silly. It suits you."

When her eyes met his, a surge of passion thundered over Michael without warning and he leaned over and pulled her into his arms, settling his lips over hers as he wrapped his arms around her. Kylah moaned and leaned into him, returning his kiss with a heat he'd never felt before from any woman. Within an instant, the flame blazed white-hot, blocking all rational thought from Michael's mind.

Without warning, she jerked away and shoved him hard enough to push him onto his back.

"This isn't some fairy tale and I'm not some bimbo you can charm out of her land." In one move, she was on her feet and gone, disappearing into the trees like Cinderella fleeing the ball.

"What the hell…"

Michael couldn't breathe. He wasn't sure if it was from the kiss or the vacuum created when Kylah wrenched herself from his arms. He got to his feet and absent-mindedly searched the ground for a glass slipper he was fairly certain he wouldn't find. Like a man drugged, he stumbled toward the ranch just as his watch struck midnight.

From behind a tree, a woman stood in the dark and observed him through bright green eyes. Her watch softly chimed midnight. She smiled and patted the large gray dog on the head as he pressed tightly against her thigh.

Things were working out just as she'd planned.

The darkness in the house settled over Michael like a familiar blanket and his mind cleared as he made his way up the stairs. He wanted desperately to talk to Kylah, but something told him that would be a huge mistake. Tomorrow he'd go into town and make arrangements to do something about the river property. Then he'd find another housekeeper and have Kylah back on her own ranch by dinnertime.

Although part of him wanted keep her here, that wasn't possible. She hated him. She would never trust him. It was time he admitted this arrangement had been a mistake. The faster he had her out of his house, the better off they would both be.

Kylah crept down the stairs with suitcase in hand, determined to be home before anyone discovered she was gone. Moving in with Michael Beasty had been a real mistake, one that threatened her heart more than she could stand. Last night had been a wake-up call. There must be another way to save her ranch.

Sometime in the wee hours, Kylah had finally admitted to herself she'd fallen for the man. A handsome face and dark gray eyes had captured her heart when her mind knew him for the devil in disguise. Her cheeks burned with shame. How could she betray her family? She'd gone in league with the enemy and now her heart was lost.

Tiptoeing out the front door, Kylah almost fell over the big dog stretched across the doorway like a dirty gray braided rug.

"Going somewhere?"

Kylah jumped. "Holy crap!" she whispered loudly, desperate not to wake anyone. Her heart hammered in her chest. "You scared me half to death."

Delta Jane sat regally on the bench next to the door, quietly staring at Kylah through long black lashes that had to be artificial.

She squinted. Delta looked blue in the dark dawn light.

Blue clothes, blue hat, blue hair, and Kylah had no doubt her eyes would be blue.

"Your hair's gonna fall out if you keep doing that."

With a throaty chuckle, Delta shrugged. "Never happen." She stared hard at the suitcase. "Turning tail and running home? What about your ranch?"

Kylah blinked. How did she know about her ranch? Michael must've told her. Standing straight and hitching the strap of her bag higher up on her shoulder, Kylah started across the porch and down the steps. "I don't know. I'll figure something out."

"You love him, you know."

"Doesn't matter."

"He loves you."

"Not a chance."

Nothing more was said as Kylah threw her bag in the back and hopped in the truck. A lump slammed her throat shut as she turned the key in the ignition and put the truck in gear. She drove down the lane, tears filling her eyes, as she watched Delta and the dog grow smaller in her rearview mirror.

Michael entered the kitchen and switched the light on. No Kylah, no pots on the stove. Instinctively, he knew she'd gone, but he went to the front door and stepped onto the porch to look anyway.

"She's gone," came Delta's voice from the bench.

"And yet, you're still here...and your little dog too."

"Told you, he's your dog now."

"And I told you I don't want that damn dog."

"But you do want Kylah, don't you?"

Michael was quiet for a moment as he scanned the horizon. She was out there somewhere, and she hated him.

"Doesn't matter." He turned back into the house and let the door slam shut behind him.

Kylah jumped and her head snapped up at the loud pounding on the door.

"Kylah! Kylah, open the door. You've got to see this," her

father's voice carried through the door. Kylah, open up!"

Slowly, she made her way to the door and unlocked it. Since leaving the Double-B early this morning, she'd buried herself in paperwork all day, hoping to find something, anything, to help her save their ranch. Nothing. No bucket of money squirreled away and forgotten, no accounting error in their favor, nothing that yielded enough money to buy back the land.

Kylah tried to smile as she opened the door. "What's so exciting?"

Outside in the hallway, her father bounced on his toes, ecstatic about something. "Look, look here. You won't believe this. Look!" He waved an envelope in her face frantically, his long gray comb-over flapping up and down as he hopped from one foot to the other, pale green eyes big and round.

"Daddy, calm down. What is it?" Impatiently, she batted at his hand.

"The land. It's the river land. It's ours again. We haven't lost it."

She stared at him. Had he completely lost his mind? She sighed. Might be a blessing father didn't completely understand what he'd done.

"Okay, Daddy, show me what you've got."

He stopped bouncing and held the envelope out in front of him like a small child with a good report card. "Here. Look."

Kylah took it and pulled out a set of legal papers. She stared at the contract in her hand. After reading the first paragraph several times, the meaning finally registered.

"Was I right, Kylah? Was I? Are we okay?"

She nodded as her eyes filled with tears. "Yes, Daddy, you were right. Michael has put the land into trust, in both names. He's given the McCombs and the Beastys joint ownership. Neither of us can sell the property without approval from both parties."

A sob wrenched itself from her throat as Kylah realized she'd been wrong about Michael Beasty. "Oh, Daddy, I've been such a fool."

At the sound of a throaty laugh behind her, Kylah spun in

the doorway to the office.

"Delta?"

With a smile, the arrogant old woman slipped past and took her father's arm. "Come on, Willy, let's leave Kylah to decide how to make it up to Michael Beasty."

Preening like a teenager on his first date and wearing a grin fit to split his face in two, Kylah's father Willy licked his right hand and smoothed it across the disheveled comb-over before leading Delta down the hallway.

"Wait!" Kylah looked over her shoulder at the room behind her. There was no other door and the window had been painted shut a year ago.

"How the hell did you get in there?"

Delta Jane continued down the hallway arm in arm with Kylah's father when she looked back and smiled. "Girlie, I told you before. I popped in."

Kylah stared. Popped in? Is that even possible? She looked back at the room again and whispered to herself, "It can't be. I don't even want to think about it."

A split second later, Kylah was on a dead run. She didn't know where they came from, but her truck keys were in her hand and she knew where she needed to be.

❦

Michael sat at the kitchen table with a bottle of whiskey in his left hand, a full shot glass in his right. He heard a truck in the driveway, but didn't move. Probably one of the ranch hands heading into town. The front door slammed and he swore.

"Damn, a man can't even get drunk around here."

He tossed back the shot and before the glass even hit the table, he'd poured another, sloshing whiskey over the edge of the shot glass and onto the tablecloth.

As he slammed back the next shot, a woman's voice startled him, causing him to choke on the whiskey against the back of his throat.

"Real nice! I'm gone one day and already you're drunk."

Michael's head swung around. Kylah. God, she was beautiful. But she couldn't be here, not really. He blinked.

Maybe it was the whiskey. She was still there.

In two steps, she crossed the room and stood in front of him. This was no figment of his imagination and the heart hammering inside his chest knew it.

He couldn't speak, couldn't move. He stared as Kylah hitched one leg over his thigh and settled on his lap to face him.

"You came back," he managed to whisper. "You're really here."

Kylah smiled and gave a wicked chuckle. "Yeah, and from the looks of it, I'm just in time. Someone's going to have to keep an eye on you."

As the blood reached Michael's brain, he grinned, but didn't move. "Yeah, you never know what might happen if I'm left alone without adult supervision."

Kylah leaned in close enough for Michael to feel her breath on his face. "Well, we can't take any chances, can we?"

Before she could move or change her mind, Michael wrapped his arms around her and crushed her to his chest, claiming her lips.

"Ahem." The voice came from the doorway. Delta Jane.

Kylah opened her eyes, but didn't move her lips from Michael's. He stared into her eyes and felt her grin against his lips.

"You two gonna come up for air any time soon?"

They turned to find Delta standing in the doorway, still blue from head to toe. Brutus leaned against her side looking, if possible, dirtier than ever. There were twigs and sticks tightly matted into the dreadlocks. Michael made a mental note to give the dog a haircut and a bath.

"I like the blue," said Kylah.

Delta glanced down and puffed out her almost flat chest, smoothing the front of her shirt. "Yeah, I like it too. I'm thinking about getting a boob job." She looked up and a smile lit her face as her sky-blue eyes twinkled. "Whaddayathink?"

Michael couldn't help but laugh. She might be as crazy as they come, but the old woman was a real hoot.

"Aren't you a little...uh...well, old for a boob job?" Kylah looked like she was struggling not to laugh herself.

Bright blue eyes narrowed and fixed on Kylah. "Old? Girlie, I'll have you know, three-hundred twenty-seven is the prime of life for an FGM. Besides, someone has to keep that smart-ass Godfather busy. It sure is hell being the responsible one."

When Delta turned to go, Kylah was quick to ask, "Where you going?" Michael was surprised at the note of near-desperation in her voice.

Delta pivoted back and smiled. "Don't worry, girlie, I'll be around. Just tell Brutus if you ever need me." With a loud pop, she disappeared.

"What the…" Michael almost dumped Kylah on the floor when he surged to his feet. Steadying her as she got her feet planted, he asked, "Did you see that?"

Kylah didn't speak. She seemed frozen in place as Michael rushed to the front room. Pushing the screen door open, he expected to hear the sound of a motorcycle or be pelted with flying gravel. Nothing. Just a quiet, sleepy country lane and birds chirping in the trees.

"She's gone," he told Kylah when he returned to the kitchen.

"What? Whaddayamean gone?"

"Gone. Poof. Pop. Gone."

Kylah dropped into the chair Michael had been sitting in earlier. "You don't suppose she was telling the truth about being my FGM?"

Michael stared. "FGM?"

Kylah met his eyes as she whispered, "Fairy Godmother."

They looked at each other in silence, neither of them willing to mention what was most likely going through each of their minds.

Just then, Brutus trotted into the middle of the room, his silky, shiny gray coat flowing out behind him like some fancy English Sheepdog at the Westminster dog show. Flopping to his belly with his squeaky clean fur feathered out across the wooden floor, he turned big brown eyes toward them and whined as he dropped his enormous head onto his paws.

Michael and Kylah could only stare as a deep, throaty chuckle reverberated through the kitchen.

Apparently, this *was* the stuff of fairy tales.

The End

Kayce Lassiter refers to her contemporary romance stories as "Chick Lit in Cowgirl Boots".

Visit her on the web at: www.kaycelassiter.com

Fortune's Guardian

Liddy Midnight

*A tale (loosely) inspired by 'Snow-White and
Rose-Red' by the Brothers Grimm*

You let them build a plant on our land? Our childhood stomping grounds?" Arthur Bernard punctuated the words by stomping across his brother's office. The thick carpeting reduced his footsteps to mere thumps. So much for making his point.

"Just fifteen acres of it. The parking lots are below grade and the entire complex is as green as it gets." Conrad steepled his fingers and sighed. "Think of it as a means of paying our property taxes, and maybe much more than that. In addition to the lease payments Bernard Corporation receives—and may I remind you that you still own fifty percent—we're in line for a hefty portion of their profits."

Something in Con's voice aroused Arthur's suspicions. He kept the scowl in place and turned to face his brother. "And? There's always more with you. Why do I get the feeling that's why you're delighted I came home right now?"

Con slapped a hand over his heart and mugged dismay. "You wound me! That I might have ulterior motives rather than sheer brotherly love."

"Cut the happy horseshit. I know you too well." He slumped into a chair by the desk. "What's up with this company?"

Con straightened up in his huge desk chair and grinned. "Now that you mention it, I could use your help."

Arthur ran a hand through his hair. He hadn't been in town long enough to get it cut. He'd been thinking he might just let it grow, leaving before he had time to visit the town's barber. From the gleam in Con's eye, plans had changed. Despite his protests, he'd do whatever his brother wanted. Family, at least theirs, stuck together. "I knew it. And I'll bet five bucks I'm not the right guy for the assignment."

"Nonsense! You're perfect. You're handy and even better, you're free!"

"Not this time. You pay my standard hourly wage or I'm outta here. I've got a waiting list of paying customers."

"Done! You'll start tomorrow."

"Doing what?"

"Replacing the ballasts in all of the light fixtures. I said they're required to be green, and technology has moved on in the past six months."

"Con, I'm a mountain surveyor. You can get any electrician at half my price."

"I know I can, but that's just a cover. You'll have to get into every office, every cubicle and every lab."

He grimaced. Con never missed an opportunity to shift unpleasant or tedious tasks onto someone else. He'd bet their sister Ursula was working on something equally as mundane. The fact that she hadn't mentioned it the evening before meant she was up to her slender shoulders in this, too. "I'm the wrong guy for this."

"No, you're not. You're perfect. Your, er, unusual abilities will prove invaluable. Besides which, you're tall enough to see over cubicle walls without stretching."

Art snorted. "Flattery will get you nowhere. We have the same genes, Con, so why aren't you doing this?"

"Because they know me. You're a complete stranger and thus invisible."

"Look at the size of me! You just said I'm abnormally tall." Arthur spread his arms and loomed over his brother. "Invisible?"

Con waved a hand in dismissal. "Service people always are. Perfect for snooping."

Arthur raised an eyebrow. "Snooping for what?"

"For the past year, our competitors have been showing up with identical marketing campaigns. Not just one, once. It's happened repeatedly. Too many clients tell us our proposals just aren't up to our usual standards, because Emerald or Tesoro is offering them the same deal—and at a lower price."

Arthur shook his head. Sheesh, who was naming these companies, unimaginative sixth graders who saw a cash cow? Must be staffed by them, too, if corporate espionage was this blatant.

"Since your involvement, you say. Any leaks here?"

"Yeah, right, I've got four people working for me, and none of them has access to this kind of stuff. You think Judy or Matt has suitable contacts?"

Arthur had to grin. He could not see grandmotherly Judy, who had been with them since they started what had grown into a far-reaching conglomerate, in her tailored dresses and button earrings, shopping for a buyer for high-tech secrets. She ran a mean spreadsheet, but only for numbers sent in by their independent divisions. Calculations she knew. Competitors' management or how to approach them with illicit information, no way.

The same went for Matt, their acquisitions expert. He wasn't as prim as Judy but he was a long-time employee and as honest as they came. Julia, Conrad's new personal assistant, had joined the staff only a few weeks earlier.

Con grinned back. "You see. It's got to be someone at Fortune Pharma."

"Tell me what kinds of things I'm looking for. What's been duplicated in your competitors' presentations—do you think ad concepts are being transferred? Or is it more technical than that? Maybe we should start with what Fortune Pharma does."

"Fortune Pharma started off as a data mining company. They then expanded into document management and electronic archiving. Now we've got a new product, and I fully expect to run into a similar one being offered by either Emerald or Tesoro. When senior staff saw how inept the clinical packaging industry was at some filling processes, they—"

"I'm the wrong guy for this. My eyes are glazing over. Give me the one-minute pitch and then something concrete I can sniff out."

"One minute pitches are easy. A nephew of one of the Fortune principals designed a robot for a school project that answers a costly problem in processing drug materials."

Arthur whistled. "And that got leaked? They're sunk!"

"Along with some marketing campaigns and ad designs, the software to run the robot has gotten out. Not all but a few critical portions of the code, enough to blow our advantage. You're right about the situation looking bleak—unless we can prove who's involved. That's where you come in."

"Does it extend beyond Emerald and Tesoro?"

"No, thank God. Most people don't know that Tesoro holds a sizable interest in Emerald, so what one has, they both have."

❧

Arthur flipped open the electrical panel cover and grimaced. "I'm the wrong guy for this." He said it before and he'd say it again, although this time there was no one to hear. His words sank into the executive suite's thick drapes and plush furniture.

His brother had heard, but he hadn't listened.

'Green' office space wasn't quite what Arthur expected. Sisal carpeting, potted plants everywhere, many windows and open stairways gave every appearance of modern comfort. He could imagine sitting amidst the bustle of coworkers while he got a lot done. The space just felt good.

But how was he supposed to snoop when every drawer he'd tried so far was locked up tight? Opportunity for snooping was no problem. He'd only seen two people. The receptionist painting her nails at the front desk and the guy cleaning the men's room weren't high on his list of suspects.

Elevator doors opened behind him, with a whisper of sound and a change in air pressure. He cocked his head. The click-click of heels in the tile hall almost drowned out the sound of a woman's pleasant voice.

Not likely the perp he'd been sent to find. In his experience, criminals skulked into their target areas. They didn't announce their presence by talking to themselves. A second female voice responded, making it unlikely he'd get anything useful to Conrad from these women.

He resumed his examination of the wires but didn't relax. His muscles tightened under his borrowed coveralls. He realized that he knew that voice. He also knew the feminine scent that reached him on the slight breeze from the HVAC system.

Bianca Fortuna. And her sister Rosa. A distraction he didn't need.

The executive offices bore no identification. He hadn't connected the dream girl of his youth with the hi-tech corporation his brother was financing. Dammit. Con should have given him the whole story.

His goals shifted and realigned with the speed of thought. He no longer just needed to find the perp his brother wanted rooted out. He had to disengage himself from the whole situation. Quickly. Before he screwed things up. There were reasons he'd adored Bianca from afar, secrets that he couldn't afford to reveal.

He steeled himself against reacting to her appearance. Long legs, luscious breasts, long blonde hair, porcelain-pale skin, blue eyes that could drown a man. He had fallen in love with a gangly teen and kept tabs on her over the years. Not that she ever knew.

They'd always been, and always would be, worlds apart.

Bianca almost ran into the electrician hunched over the switch plate. A tiny gasp of surprise escaped her and she barely managed to stay on her feet. Rosa stopped hard on her heels.

He straightened, turning to face them.

She looked up—and up, and up. Holy mackerel, the guy topped six feet, by a long shot. More than simply tall, he was massive. Broad shoulders spread above a muscled chest. His waist wasn't too narrow. Nor were his hips. No six-pack abs here, but she'd bet his uniform concealed just the right amount of warm, solid flesh to satisfy any woman. All in all, great eye candy.

His lips quirked and she realized she'd been staring.

Meeting his gaze—who really had eyes that soulful brown?—she managed to speak without having to clear her throat. "Mister—" She glanced down at the name embroidered on his shirt. "Kevin."

"Just Kevin's fine, ma'am." Humor laced his rough voice.

The deep timbre sent a shiver down her spine.

"I'm Bianca." She stuck out her hand and his engulfed it briefly. "And this is my sister, Rosa."

"Pleased to meet you." He slipped a screwdriver into his chest pocket. "I'll come back when you're done."

She waved a hand, indicating he should stay put. "No need. You may have noticed that there's nobody around right now. Today and tomorrow, we're taking advantage of the nice weather to conduct some team-building exercises outdoors."

"Outside? All of you?"

"Yes, all of the professional staff. You don't have to worry about disturbing anyone. Production is still operating and I'd prefer our maintenance staff perform those upgrades. Up here, you're on your own. We're essentially closing down the business end of things for today and tomorrow."

"Just for two days?"

"Can't afford longer than that."

He nodded. "Gotcha."

Rosa poked her in the ribs and hissed, "Let's get the stuff we need and go."

Bianca yanked her attention off the hunky electrician. It wasn't easy. "Stopwatches and time sheets are here." She opened a credenza drawer and pulled out a box. "The sacks for the first race are down at the security desk. Prizes aren't needed until we wrap up tomorrow over the final barbecue. Anything else?"

Leading her out by the arm, Rosa whispered with a jerk of her head, "How about that yummy hunk? I could eat him for dinner."

"Me, too." Bianca gave her sister the required response, but something about Kevin niggled at her. He seemed familiar, although she knew she'd never met him. Surely she'd remember those eyes, the color of sinful, dark chocolate. Yummy, indeed.

The hum of an electric wheelchair interrupted their trip to the elevator. Bianca frowned as one of her assistants wheeled out of an office.

"Elaine! Everyone's supposed to be outdoors. What are

you doing here?"

"My job." The petite brunette scowled. "I figured I could get a leg up on the backlog over the next two days."

Bianca took a deep breath. Try as she might, she had trouble liking Elaine. The woman was capable but had a chip on her shoulder the size of Mount Elbert. "You're a valued part of the team. What makes you think you're not expected to play with the rest of us?"

"Look at me!" With a sweep of her hand, Elaine indicated her chair. "What am I gonna do? Climb ropes? Run through the woods? You're probably including me because of some anti-discrimination thing, but I decline. It's not happening."

"There are paved paths, which you'd know if you ever bothered to look beyond your own misery. Just because you're not ambulatory doesn't mean you get to sit out. I expect you downstairs in fifteen minutes. You *will* participate, Elaine."

Bianca didn't hang around for a response.

Rosa steered her toward the elevator. "Get your blood pressure down, sis."

Bianca counted off the floors on the elevator's display. What she needed right now was a nice, long walk in the woods. At just the thought of strolling down the shady paths, her pulse began to slow. She rubbed the back of her neck and sighed. "I hate losing my temper like that."

"She needed it. She doesn't even try to fit in. Everyone barely tolerates her."

"Personality is no reason to fire the handicapped and she knows it. Unfortunately, she's a good worker." Never in her life had she thought to say those words. Until Elaine joined their staff, she'd prized every competent employee.

"Con," Arthur growled into his cell phone. "You're cleared for this job. Building's empty."

Con's voice crackled over the connection. "What?"

"They're all outdoors, playing Blind Man's Bluff and singing campfire songs. Some corporate bonding crap. I've got better things to do." And better things to watch. Like Bianca Fortuna hitching up her shorts and wading through the stream, like she did back when she was sixteen.

Bianca's scent lingered on his hand. He inhaled it, knowing he'd never get enough. Maybe he could get close to her again. Once upon a time, he'd easily gotten inside her natural defenses, playing on her innocence. Over the years, she'd spent endless days frolicking through the mountain woods and streams. Maybe there was still some childish innocence lurking inside that knockout woman.

Only what he wanted now wasn't innocent at all. He'd much rather she rubbed some other body parts of his.

Get a grip. This job was over. He snapped the case shut and gathered his tools. On the way to the elevator, an irritated snort reminded him of his snooping task. He was still here, and he might as well do what Con wanted him to, at least until he could hand off the job to his brother.

A woman in a wheelchair struggled with a briefcase, a satchel and a couple of small containers while trying to close an office door. The boxes slid off and sent a glittering cascade of DVDs across the carpet. "Damn!"

"Let me help you, ma'am."

"Be careful!" she snapped. Something about her raised the hair on the back of his neck.

Arthur gingerly began picking up the disks. On a hunch, he pushed one behind a large potted plant. If Con decided it wasn't important, he'd return it tomorrow.

"I hope they're not scratched, you big oaf."

Arthur recoiled at the venom in her voice. Once he'd filled both boxes, he helped restore balance to her load—careful not to touch her—and shut the office door.

Hostility so intense it was almost palpable poured off her, filling the hallway. She ignored him, pointedly checking the stack atop the briefcase on her lap. The beast within him growled and pushed for release.

He left her at the elevator and took the stairs before he did something he'd regret.

Concealed by underbrush, secure in the knowledge that his fur blended into the shadows, Arthur watched the Fortune

Pharma employees and a few of their families split into yet another set of teams. He had to admire the Fortuna sisters for their organization skills and their determination to include everyone in the games.

The woman in the wheelchair objected to everything. From his position, he could hear her try to opt out of the water balloon toss. She bitched as Rosa produced a plastic sheet to protect her clothing and chair. Even winning the three-legged race—with someone's toddler standing on her footrests—didn't improve her mood.

Bianca continually drew his attention. She had blossomed in their years apart. The promise of beauty she'd shown as a teen had come true. He'd know her anywhere. No matter what she was doing or where she went, despite the company ball cap that hid her distinctive hair, he picked her out of the crowd with ease.

The smell of cooking meat made his stomach growl. He debated the wisdom of creeping closer to the barbecue pit. He doubted he could snag anything without being noticed but it would be one hell of an adrenaline rush to try.

That was a thought he had to squelch. Yeah, he was hungry but he wasn't about to call attention to himself that way. Or disrupt the Fortune Pharma company picnic or whatever the hell this was.

He shoved his hunger aside and kept watch.

"This was a great idea," Bianca said. "Everyone's having a good time, and they're talking about things other than their jobs. Getting to know their coworkers better is helping them see each other as something more than a job description."

"Yeah, everyone should go back to work on Thursday energized." Rosa looked across the busy picnic tables and smiled. "We'll have to do something nice to thank Mary for the suggestion and for helping with the plans."

All but the last few race-walkers had checked in. Bianca peered down the trail but saw no sign of anyone. The event had been going so smoothly, too. Maybe she should make sure no one had turned an ankle. All they needed to dampen the day was an injury.

She nudged her sister. "I'm going to make a quick sweep around the course. Be back in a few minutes."

Rosa nodded. "Good idea. You can haul in the stragglers, boss lady."

Thank God for sisters. No one knew her better. They had spent every childhood vacation at nearby campgrounds. She and Rosa had roamed through these woods for a month every summer until they both knew every gully and every fox den. When the opportunity appeared to build her dream facility here, she grabbed it. What better place than in the paradise of her childhood?

The only thing missing was *him.*

Her thoughts frequently turned to what might have become of the young bear that they had gotten to know. He'd most likely been reared in a wildlife rescue station, because he had no fear of humans. Well, no fear of her or of Rosa.

Barely half-grown when they first saw him, he'd rolled on the ground, just begging to be petted. Initially frozen with fear, she'd been the first to venture to touch him. After that first meeting, he'd appeared almost every day.

In the last year, she'd walked for miles, off the trails, deep into the wilds they'd explored together so long ago, and never saw any sign of him. Sometimes she could swear he was out there, watching—in fact, she had that feeling today—but she never saw him. Rosa teased her about her affinity for the woods but not even her sister knew how deep Bianca's interest was. It was almost as if speaking about it would destroy the magic. If that happened, she was afraid she'd never find him.

She didn't want to think about what her near-obsession said about her. She was a grown woman now, and should accept the dinner invitations her lawyer's partner made every time they met. Corporate executives weren't supposed to be most comfortable wandering the woods.

Up ahead, where the trail looped back to the Fortune Pharma campus, something glinted in the sun. Leaves shifting in the breeze made dappled shade that came and went along with the glitter. She picked up her pace.

An abandoned wheelchair sat in the grass just off the trail— Elaine's, the last thing she expected to see. The brake was set. Elaine's briefcase, which she had kept tucked by her side even during the most active games, and her huge tote were gone, along with Elaine.

But to where? Elaine wasn't registered for the walking race. Bianca couldn't imagine a reason for Elaine to be out here in the first place, let alone off the trail and on foot.

She examined the area, distracting herself from thoughts of what another of her employees, goaded by Elaine's acid tongue, might have done.

The undergrowth around the chair wasn't trampled. There was no sign of a fight, or of a crippled woman being dragged away against her will. It looked as if Elaine had just walked off.

That was impossible.

Elaine's legs had been mangled in an accident two years ago and she'd been told she would never walk again. HR had the disability reports.

She was petite; a man might have scooped her up and left no sign. Maybe for a romantic tryst? Bianca almost laughed, despite her worries. No way could she see Elaine cuddled in a lover's arms. The woman was as prickly as a porcupine.

She must have been taken against her will. Bianca glanced back, toward the picnic tables, where everyone else waited for the Last Place winner. Should she get help? Time might be a critical factor. She stepped off the tarmac and into the underbrush, determined to find her missing employee.

Arthur lumbered along, paralleling the paved trail. He'd known the instant Bianca left the picnic and followed. A guilty pleasure, one that took him back in time. She'd filled out, into womanly curves that only made her more attractive. His mouth watered. He'd thought the aroma of barbecue was tempting. The prospect of tasting Bianca's skin was more heady than honey. And everyone knows how bears love honey.

His huge paws made little noise on the thick loam. He followed a deer path, keeping low to avoid twigs and branches that might snap and give him away.

He knew where she was headed. A natural basin, formed over the years by pooled snowmelt, made a natural clearing. Several fallen trees at one edge provided seating.

Ahead, unfamiliar voices rose in anger.

Bianca got there before he did. He ducked into the shade of a small fir to watch without being seen.

Crap. The crippled woman who'd dropped the disks in the hallway stood in the center of the clearing, with her wheelchair nowhere in sight. A man—not anyone he recognized—pulled the woman in an embrace.

Or did he? Was his arm held around her neck in affection or in anger? Had he interrupted a lovers' spat or a serious argument?

He took in the rest of the scene. Elaine's open briefcase sat on the nearest log. The contents of her tote spilled across the grass.

Bianca stepped into the sunlight. "Elaine! Are you all right?"

Elaine started to respond but the man jerked his arm and choked off her words.

Bianca moved closer to the couple. "What's the matter, James, didn't you find what you want?"

"No, Miss Fortuna, I have exactly what I came for." He patted Elaine on the head. "My little friend here could have been useful for a lot longer, but she's grown greedy. She wants a position of responsibility at Emerald."

"She's a good worker. You could do worse."

"I couldn't trust her. She's been selling out your company for months." He patted a pocket. "I've got the rest of the automation code, all I need to eat your lunch."

"James, you don't watch enough television. You should know what a slim chance anyone has of getting away with computer crimes. Every keystroke leaves a trail. I'm surprised you lost sight of that, since you started off as a programmer."

Good girl, keep him talking. Arthur worked his way around the outskirts of the clearing as Bianca lectured on the value of some television shows.

"Besides that, you're trespassing."

"That's the least of my sins." He shoved Elaine at Bianca and pulled a revolver.

Elaine scurried behind Bianca and cowered there, holding Bianca in place between her and the threat.

James scowled. "I hadn't planned to kill anyone, but I'm sure I can drag your bodies far enough that you'll be bear bait long before you're found."

Arthur didn't hesitate. He launched from his hiding place like a massive, furred missile. No one had time to react before he plowed into James, his mass carrying both of them clean across and out of the clearing.

He'd intended to knock the gun free, but somehow the perp kept a tight grip on it. He got a shot off as Arthur slammed him into the trunk of a large oak tree. James sagged onto the ground, unconscious or perhaps dead but definitely no longer a threat.

Arthur rose to return to the women. He staggered as pain blossomed in his head.

"No!" Bianca screamed as the bear stumbled and fell in a flurry of leaves.

It had to be him. It had to.

He couldn't be dead. He couldn't.

She started forward, to go to his aid, when a tug on her waistband nearly pulled her off her feet.

"Help me!" Elaine's face was ghostly pale. Her hand shook when she reached up to push her hair out of her eyes.

"Help you? You're fired and you're going to be arrested. Help yourself!" Bianca disentangled Elaine's fingers from her belt and shoved her back down.

As she hurried forward, the bear sat up and shook its head. Much like a person would do after a blow. To her dismay, blood spattered from a wound running from one ear down the back of its neck.

The shaking of its head slowed.

Her steps faltered. What if this wasn't her bear? What if she was about to try to touch a wild animal? She decided it was worth the risk. The animal was clearly disoriented. She should be able to outrun a dazed bear.

Actually, all she had to do was outrun Elaine.

Holding her breath, Bianca knelt beside the furry beast and laid her hand on its muzzle. It ducked its great head to rub its uninjured ear against her palm.

Her breath blew out in a gust of relief. She sat back on her heels and dug into a pocket. "Wait a minute, I've got a napkin or something." She pulled out a packet of tissues, tore it open and began dabbing at the blood on the bear's head. "It's not that bad. Just a groove, not very deep, and your skull's still thick enough to protect that little bear-brain." She deliberately used a phrase she and Rosa had often teased him with all those years ago.

The bear opened its mouth and barked what sounded suspiciously like a laugh. Her heart sped up.

Voices rang through the trees. She had only moments before the entire Fortune Pharma crowd arrived.

She resisted the urge to throw her arms around him.

The bear rose to its feet, towering over her. Bianca looked up and into familiar, rich, dark brown eyes. The eyes of the bear-friend of her youth.

"I'll come to see you. Will you be here?"

She swore the bear nodded before it turned and shambled into the bushes.

"Bianca, are you all right?" Rosa led the group of employees, all of whom were armed with baseball bats, golf clubs and a few folding chairs.

They gathered around her, staring at the still-unconscious James.

"Is that who I think it is? What's he doing here?"

"Why is Elaine walking on her own?"

"Holy crap, Bianca, was that a real bear?"

She bit her tongue to keep from saying something smart-ass. She slid back in boss mode, calming the excited picnickers.

Once James was bound with belts and Elaine similarly secured in her wheelchair, they all trekked back to meet the local constabulary at the company's drive.

Bianca brought up the rear, casting one last, longing look back into the trees.

꙰

For the next two weeks, she visited the clearing every day. She took a book to read and stayed at least an hour each time.

For the next two weeks, there was no sign of her bear.

Late one morning, her cell phone rang as she headed out of her office. Rosa. "Hey, sis."

"Are you still obsessing over that bear?"

"I wouldn't call it 'obsessing'." Geez, that made it sound like something a psychotherapist would have a field day with. She wasn't sure just what this was all about, but she couldn't deny the fascination. Even more, now that he'd acted so, well, human. Long past the age of believing he might be an enchanted prince, she was nonetheless drawn to him.

"I would. And you'd better stop at Reception on your way out. You've got a visitor." Rosa's voice held a smug smile. "I can see him from my inner window. Yummy."

Damn. She'd forgotten she'd asked the electrician, who'd managed to bag some crucial evidence against Elaine and James, to stop by so she could thank him in person. That shouldn't take long. Maybe she could brush him off with a few words and be done with him.

The very tall, very broad man lumbered over to her in the lobby. She'd forgotten just how good-looking he was. She tucked the book under her arm and stuck out her hand. He enveloped it with both of his. Warmth flowed up her arm from his firm, confident grip. Definitely yummy. Maybe she didn't want to get rid of him that quickly. She was sure Rosa would say a hunky man in your hand is worth more than an elusive bear in the woods.

"It's good to see you again, Kevin."

His mouth tilted up at one corner. "No Mister today?"

She grinned. "No. I think we've moved beyond that."

"I hope so. And the name's not Kevin, it's Art. I borrowed the shirt." He still held her hand. Tingles of warmth—or maybe warning—lingered under his touch. There was something intriguing about this man. She still had the feeling she knew him.

"Really? I can't imagine where you found another

electrician who wears your size."

"It's a long story."

"I'd like to hear it." To her surprise, it was true. She was interested. She waved her free hand toward the doors. "I'm about to go for a walk. Want to come with me, and tell me your long story?"

He smiled at her. She froze as she looked into his dark chocolate-brown eyes.

The same color as her bear's.

The lobby tilted and the floor shifted beneath her feet. She closed her eyes to steady her senses. When she opened them, he still stood there and his eyes were still that unmistakable color.

Art tugged on Bianca's hand. "I know a place where we can sit and talk." Her scent, this close and strong, was intoxicating.

He held the door for her. As she stepped past him, he thought she whispered, "So do I."

Without speaking, hand in hand, they made their way past the picnic tables to the paved trail. He scanned the tree line. He cocked his head and without thinking said, "It looks different from this side."

"What?"

Ah, crap. He'd forgotten to keep his mouth shut. She didn't know the truth yet. He hoped he didn't lose his nerve.

"I roam these woods a lot. They've been in my family for generations."

"You're related to Conrad?"

"His brother. He hired me to work on the lights so I could snoop around, try to find your mole." He held his breath, waiting for her reaction. That morning, when he realized he couldn't keep away from her, he knew he had to come clean with everything.

"You said it was a long story."

He couldn't keep his lips from twitching up in a rueful smile. "It's longer than you can imagine."

She checked her watch. "I've got about an hour."

"That should give us a good start. I'm free to continue over dinner, if you're interested once the hour's up."

"That sounds ominous."

He shrugged. "I'm willing to take the risk." And it was one hell of a risk. One he'd never taken before. One he'd never wanted to take before. He hoped like hell he was right about her.

They reached the trampled path to the clearing. Two weeks was not enough time for the grass to recover from all the foot traffic during the investigation.

"How is the case against Elaine going?"

"Great. She turned on James like a rabid dog. He shouldn't have threatened her."

"Just as he accused her, he got greedy." She went still at his side. He held his breath. If she was as smart as he thought, she'd pick up on it right away.

"Did the DA tell you that?"

"We haven't discussed the case."

She released his hand and stepped back. "Then how did you know what he said?"

Wordlessly, he turned around and flipped his hair up, showing her the long, red welt from his ear down the back of his head. "My thick skull did protect my little bear brain."

She sat down heavily on the fallen tree. "Oh. My. God."

He dropped to his knees beside her. "Bianca, I was there. Like I've always been—"

She held up a hand. "Give me a minute."

Waiting was hell. In the following minutes, he learned what the phrase, 'my heart was in my mouth', meant.

He hoped she didn't faint. But if she did, he could creep away and pretend this hadn't happened.

No, he couldn't leave. No matter what she did right now, he was committed to what he'd started. He wanted her badly enough to pursue her, and to persuade her.

Emotions played across her face as she examined him. Fear. Disbelief. Fascination. Relief.

Relief?

"It's impossible. I can't believe it, I shouldn't believe it, but somehow I do." She reached out to cup his cheek. "So smooth.

So normal."

"At the moment."

Her eyes held many questions, but she asked simply, "How?"

"Got me." He shrugged. "Old Native American blood. Mutation. God-like genes. Who knows? Our paternal grandfather could shift but not our father. We don't know many others, but they have to be out there."

"Why me and Rosa?"

"I was thirteen that first summer, exploring my world as a bear. There are dangers in these woods. You were irresistible, just watching you and Rosa was more fun than I'd ever had. I took on the responsibility of keeping you out of trouble. I didn't have willpower, not enough to keep my distance. Just like I didn't today."

She took a deep breath and stood up. Her clear, blue eyes echoed her wide grin. Squaring her shoulders, she said, "I'd like to continue this over dinner."

Pulling her into his arms, he brushed his mouth over hers. She tasted better than he'd imagined. She melted against him.

"I think it may take a lot longer than dinner."

Her eyes sparkled and her lips curved in an enticing smile. "Whatever. I've spent too long looking for you to let you go now." She pulled him back for a deep kiss.

The End

Liddy Midnight lives, loves, works and writes in the woods of eastern Pennsylvania, surrounded by lush greenery and wildlife. Although raccoons and the occasional fox visit her yard, she's no more than half an hour from some of the finest shopping in the country. Situated in this best of all possible worlds, how could she write anything other than romance?

For excerpts and updates, visit: www.liddymidnight.com

The Unwilling Frog and the Mystery Princess

Sahara Kelly

"I look silly."

"No you don't." Sarah Morton Howe grinned at her sister. "You look fabulous. And it's only for a few hours."

Lily Morton stared at the mirror. "Sort of like Marie Antoinette got together with Tinkerbelle and swapped wardrobe concepts." She twirled the huge skirt and grimaced at the lacy wings behind her. "I can fly to my date with the guillotine."

Sarah laughed. "Goof. You've wanted to deal at the tables since you were four. If Daddy hadn't owned the place, you'd probably be there now. You know what you're doing; nobody's better at dealing blackjack than you – here's your chance. Take it. Have fun!"

Lily pulled the veil mask down over her nose and took one last peek in the mirror. "You sure you can't recognize me?"

"With all those sparkly things over your face? Mom wouldn't recognize you, Lily." Sarah patted her tummy. "I envy you. If it wasn't for your niece or nephew here, I'd be in that gown right this minute." She narrowed her eyes. "And if you're worried that Mr. *Lovely Man* is going to know who you are, don't."

Lily swallowed. "Don't tease. I simply said he was nice looking, that's all."

With the innate ability of one sister to read another, Sarah smirked. "Yes, dear."

Lily sighed. The annual Masquerade Ball at Morton's

Casino was one of the highlights of the year for everyone, staff included. When the chance to cover for one of her friends on the floor had arisen, Lily leaped at it. Being the daughter of the owner didn't exactly mean she got to mingle with people on a regular basis – Dad was too security-conscious for that. But she managed to find a few buddies amongst the slots and the tables, parent notwithstanding. And recently, a very handsome new pit boss had caught her eye.

Of course, she couldn't do anything about it, given who she was. It was a blessing and a curse. She loved her life, loved the Casino, and loved her family. But given her sister's marriage and growing family, Lily found herself wanting something of her own to love as well. Or *someone*.

Like that really, really nice looking man who kept a sharp eye on the blackjack tables...

Unbeknownst to the two girls in the penthouse, that man was, at that precise moment, staring at himself in what could best be described as abject horror.

"Dear Lord. I'm *green*."

"Sorry, Peter. It was the best I could do. You're not the easiest man to fit, you know." Tony Santiago, the go-to guy for Morton's Casino, tried not to snicker.

"Why not? I'm average, aren't I?" Peter stared at the suit he'd put on, his stomach muscles clenching as it almost blinded him. Grass would shudder if it was that color. Astroturf should be so lucky.

"Not really. You're taller than average for a start, athletically built, unlike a lot of the staff, and I got to the costume room a bit late when your call came through." Tony raised an eyebrow. "If you'd let me know a few hours earlier that you didn't have an outfit for tonight..."

Peter Macintosh winced. "I had no idea the staff were supposed to dress up for this darn thing. I'm a pit-boss, for heaven's sake. How am I supposed to look authoritative in this?" He spread his arms wide. "All I'm good for is catching flies on my tongue. I'm a frog, Tony. A complete and utter *frog!*"

Tony gave up the battle and burst out laughing. "Yeah, but you make one helluva handsome one, Boss."

Peter rolled his eyes. He was stuck and he knew it. This was his first experience with the annual extravaganza known as Morton's Masquerade, and he would be damned if he let the team down.

For once he was grateful that the beautiful daughter of the house didn't come around too often. If she ever saw him like this… well, not that there could be anything between them, but still. What gorgeous girl would even look at a frog, let alone consider *dating* one?

He reached for his mask and tied it behind his head. "This doesn't help, does it?"

Tony's laughter had subsided to the occasional chuckle. "Look, it could be worse. Harry got the chicken suit. He's going to be handling the number four roulette table and scratching his feathers at the same time. Not to mention the feet thing."

Peter shrugged. "Point taken. Although if there's ever a St. Patrick's Day gala, I'm thinking this suit will go before any of the others to some kind of overgrown leprechaun with a sequin fetish. It's just a shame this *isn't* St. Patrick's Day." He gulped. "And I still look like a frog, dammit."

Tony pulled the last item from the bag. "Here. Put this on. It'll change everything."

Peter lifted the thin gold wire crown from Tony's hand and plopped it on his head. "Oh yes. You're right. That does change *everything*." His voice was wry. "Now I'm not just a frog, I'm a damned frog *prince*."

"Go get 'em, your Highness."

"I could fire you for that."

"You won't. Frog princes are good people." Tony chuckled once more. "*Ribbit*."

"You're pushing it." Peter swung on his heel and stalked to the door, trying to ignore the swish of the green glittery tunic he wore over a green silk shirt and matching pants that were a whole lot too snug for his taste.

His gut churned and he became acutely aware of why the

color green was commonly associated with nausea. Clenching his teeth against the roiling indigestion low in his stomach, he strode as naturally as he could from his small apartment to the elevator and punched the button for the Casino floor.

So he was green. Big deal. So he looked like a frog. No big deal there, either.

Unless...unless *she* decided to show up this evening. And the way his luck was running, she probably would, too.

Peter wondered if all frogs were having a bad day or if it was just him.

On the third blackjack table from the bar, a certain costumed princess was having a ball herself.

She'd come on the floor at nine for a three-hour shift behind the shoe, knowing that she'd freed up her friend Sue, whose daughter had just come down with chicken-pox. The timing was awful for the poor child, and Lily had been more than happy to tell Sue not to worry about coming in that night. She, Lily, would make arrangements for coverage.

Sue, busy applying calamine lotion to a scratching and miserable six-year-old, wouldn't have the time to even consider the notion that her slot might be filled on this special night by the daughter of the owner!

But it was, and Lily was having the time of her life. Her fingers knew the feel and texture of playing cards as well as they knew her own face. She'd been raised around them, learned to count using them, and was regularly beating her family at blackjack before she could legibly write her name.

Craps was something alien to her, roulette bored her, poker was too much work, and the slots – well, her first piggy bank was a miniature slot machine, so there wasn't much fun to be had there.

Nope, it was blackjack that was Lily's passion, and tonight? Well, tonight she was exploring the true excitement of that passion by sharing it with real, honest-to-God players who had no idea who she was.

Her heart thundered with each slap of her fingers on the shoe, each card that slid smoothly across the table, each colorful face she turned up on her own line. She stood on sixteen and drew on seventeen without a hitch, paid off blackjacks, scooped up losing bets and did it all with adrenaline flowing through her veins and a smile showing widely beneath her mask.

"You're good, honey." The housewife from Oklahoma, improbably dressed as Mata Hari, grinned at her, even though this was the third hand in a row she'd lost.

"Why thank you, Ma'am." Lily smiled back. "You gonna try again?"

"Of course. But just one more hand. Then I have to go find hubby. Probably eyeing those showgirls again." She shrugged and then giggled. "Can't say as I blame him, though. You ever dance?"

Lily blinked. "Me? Lord no. Too much like exercise for my taste." There was no reason to share her daily workouts in the hotel gym or the jogs she liked to take when she got chance to head out of town to their home in the desert.

The conversation around the table became general and Lily dealt another hand, paying out two Blackjacks, helping one new player double down and making them all laugh as she busted out. She found herself more and more at home in her costume, the elegant Renaissance gown an effective screen to hide behind, the lace at her elbows fluttering as she dealt the cards and the glittering necklace a cool, reassuring weight against the skin revealed by the low neckline.

It was almost as if she'd stepped into another life, become another person – thanks to some fancy-dress clothes and a mask that showed little more than her eyes to the rest of the world. She received many compliments and took them all in stride, something that was a little out of character for the shy-natured girl she usually was.

She laughed and joked freely, not worrying about what she was saying to whom or if it would reflect unfavorably on the Casino. She turned aside flirtatious comments as politely as she could.

No, she didn't want to grab a drink later with the cowboy in the white hat, nor did she want to see the Superhero's etchings. Thanks, but that wasn't permitted in the Casino.

They left the table, looking sad but not angry at having been refused. Lily figured she must be doing something right. Later, when she wasn't having so much fun, she'd try and work out what it was. But for now?

Whoooeeee!!! She was in a wonderful daze, a fantasy she'd long dreamed about, imagined several times a day – and it was so much better than anything she could have envisioned. It all seemed so natural.

And it all came to a grinding halt when something large and green blurred her peripheral vision and she glanced over to see…*him*.

⌁

Peter had managed to forget his atrocious suit as the business of the night took over the majority of his brain cells. There had been a nasty moment or two with the damned tunic and a recalcitrant bar stool, but he'd untangled himself with a minimum of damage, apologized to the stunned customer, and comped him another drink. He was happy to accept.

In keeping with his job as pit-boss, Peter had even managed to brush off the comment he'd overheard. "Hey dude. That sparkly green frog prince over there just comped me another beer."

It was all in good fun. Of *course* it was all in good fun. Peter's ego would survive being known to all and sundry as the "sparkly green frog prince".

Probably. He might have to take a few days off and make sure there wasn't one piece of green clothing in his closet, *ever*, but other than that, he'd make it until midnight, emerald sequins notwithstanding.

Fortunately, his friends weren't the sort to follow him around the casino floor making comments about flies, ponds, and amphibians in general or frogs in particular.

He even managed to ignore or summon up a chuckle at the occasional "ribbit" that echoed as he passed by. Instinct urged him to take names for later butt-kicking, but he battled it down, knowing this was a special night at Morton's and liberties could be allowed that otherwise would have brought the wrath of Peter Macintosh down on more than a few heads.

It was almost an hour before he found himself closing in on the "fun" blackjack tables, the ones where the players were two-to-ten dollar bettors, there just to enjoy themselves and try their luck.

The hairs on the back of his neck stood up as he caught his first glimpse of the woman dealing so proficiently at number three table. The one that should, by rights, have been Sue's.

It sure as hell wasn't Sue.

Peter had to force his mouth closed as he drank in the vision behind the green baize blackjack cloth.

Slender and tall, she wore some glittery golden gown that should have been preserved forever in a life-sized painting on the walls of Versailles. A large and elegant white coiled wig covered her hair, dotted here and there with something that flashed reflections of the casino lights in rainbows all over the place, dazzling the unwary.

A matching necklace adorned her neckline, cool stones against creamy skin that made Peter swallow down a most un-princely lump of need that had risen up into his throat and almost choked him. He wanted to brush a fingertip over that skin and see if it was as silky as it looked.

Her skirts swished with each move she made; the gold lace falling from her sleeves framed arms that were strong and slim. Her hands flew around the cards with the confidence of a dealer who'd done that very thing for more years than they could remember.

No, it definitely wasn't Sue, good at her job though Sue was. This woman, this *goddess*, well, she was somebody Peter couldn't quite place. But as he stared closely, trying to pierce the veil that concealed her face from his gaze, a suspicion took shape in the back of his mind.

And when she laughed, it became more than a suspicion. That light and happy sound was very familiar. It was the first thing that had attracted him to one Lily Morton.

His boss's daughter.

Oh sweet Lord. He was in trouble now, and no mistake about it.

Lily could feel his hot gaze sliding up and down her body as vividly as if he'd put his hands on her.

I wish he would.

No. Bad girl.

She was a dealer tonight, somebody whose total attention had to be on the players at her table, not the delectable six-foot or so of pit boss. Even though he was looking at her like she was a glass of iced water and he'd just been in the Nevada desert for six months licking dry rock formations.

For the first time, Lily's hands shook a little as she dealt the cards from the shoe. Thank heavens she'd shuffled and refilled the wooden device a while ago because she'd have a really hard time trying to do it with his dark eyes on her.

She knew him, of course. Even with the disguise of a rather virulent green outfit, Peter's tall good looks still shone through. Already he was getting a few "frog" comments, but to Lily he was every inch a prince first.

Okay, and frog second. That suit really did scream "pond dweller" in a loud and unavoidable tone of voice. She slid the cards face down to the players and wondered who the heck had imagined this particular man would be happy to wander the place strongly resembling a cartoonish amphibian with a headache. The headache she judged from the distinct downturn of his lips beneath his mask.

Or perhaps he'd eaten a fly that disagreed with him.

She squelched a nervous giggle and turned her thoughts more forcefully to the game. Two players had busted out already, one had doubled down, and one more was carefully hoarding two deuces and a five.

He was coming closer, closer still, making goosebumps frizzle along Lily's arms. Then he was beside her.

"Marie Antoinette, I presume?" He lifted one of her hands and kissed it politely, bringing laughter to the players at the table with his courtly gesture.

Lily's laugh strangled around her tonsils somewhere at the touch of his lips to her skin. "Uhhh…"

"I trust her Majesty is taking good care of you all?" Peter

turned his masked face to the table.

"Bet your scales, Mr. Frog." This was Vern, the would-be racing car driver from Minnesota. He fancied himself as the lord of the track, and wore a jumpsuit that was covered with every motor racing emblem produced since the dawn of time.

It barely covered Vern, since there was a lot of Vern to cover. About five hundred miles around, give or take, and probably left hand turns all the way. Lily did her best to enter the spirit of the thing and ignore the sweet burn still searing her knuckles.

"Of course, Your Highness."

See? Not everybody's doing frog jokes.

"Bet there's no flies on him." Vern's wife dug her elbow into Vern, barely making a dent in the oil filter patch.

Lily managed to avoid rolling her eyes and couldn't help a quick glance at Peter, who was doing much the same thing at exactly the same moment. *So much for the frog jokes.* Apologetically, Lily shrugged.

To her surprise, Peter grinned back. "I'm getting used to it." His gaze dropped to her neck and before she could anticipate his move, he delicately brushed a finger from her shoulder to her ear. "Keep your head, your Majesty."

"I'll try." She whispered the words even as she wondered if she could live up to them. This might well be the one man she could lose her head with, quite happily. Bring on the tumbril, the Bastille, and even the guillotine. She was soooo in trouble and almost on fire from just the thought of it.

She shivered.

"If you two don't mind, I want that last card. Gimme a winner, Queenie."

Vern's raspy voice blew the moment away in an instant and Lily blushed beneath her veil as she returned her attention to the game, dragging it with effort away from the man beside her.

She did indeed deal Vern a winner and in the general cheering and groaning that always accompanied a pure King-Ace Blackjack, Peter slipped away.

Lily felt his absence like a cold draft against her body, an empty spot she'd not known existed until he filled it. What the heck was the matter with her anyway? She was acting like some silly girl, not a grown woman. She was, of course a grown woman suffering from the lack of any important man in her life, but that was neither here nor there.

Peter was neither here nor there, either. She lost sight of him for the next hour or so, only to see an occasional twinkle of his green suit as the night wore on and he patrolled the tables under his jurisdiction.

Time seemed to fly as quickly as if it wore wings, speeding down to the midnight hour when masks would be taken off, celebrations begun, and for a moment or two, Morton's would celebrate its own personal version of New Year's Eve.

It was the Casino's way of marking another year in business and thanking its guests for their patronage. And, of course, their cash. Lily had been raised in the business and never forgot the bottom line. It had paid for her schooling, her clothing, and now her little penthouse suite where she helped her father administer the Morton Foundation funds.

Already she was planning on auctioning off her costume from tonight and putting the proceeds into the arts education program she was working on. With a sigh, she realized her dream would soon be over and she would have to return to her little world with only her memories of a night spent in a fantasy.

And having a special man drop a kiss on her hand.

Absently she lifted it to her face and brushed it against her cheek. His lips had been warm and firm...what would they feel like in a real kiss?

She would never know. It was a sad thought she tried to push away as she dealt yet another hand to her motley gathering of players. She'd had a full table all night, which was encouraging and fully justified her presence there if she had to explain it to her father.

Unfortunately, it wasn't always her skill with the cards that attracted customers to her table. This fact made itself quite plain as a new player dressed as a knight took his seat and leered at her costume, paying particular attention to her cleavage.

"Hey, beautiful Princess. I gotta *huge* castle just made for you, baby." The insidious shifting on his chair suggested more than a castle. It threw in the drawbridge as well and hinted at the size of the portcullis. "Just deal me those cards and tell me when you get off shift." He flashed a roll of chips, plunked down a couple of hundred dollars' worth and waited expectantly for his cards.

Lily gulped.

Peter had passed the time in a useless blend of efficiency and aching need. He needed to keep Lily in his sights. He had to be efficient in his monitoring of the tables. In his own mind, he was succeeding at neither task as well as he should.

Fortunately, it was a relatively quiet night for the pit-bosses. This wasn't the sort of affair that attracted too many high-rollers, but it was the kind of shindig that brought out the worst in some people.

Peter managed to calm one woman who swore her chips had been swiped by the genie sitting next to her and broke up an incipient catfight between two girls who clearly hadn't talked on the phone and ended up wearing the same costume. Their "discussion" about who looked better in it could have turned ugly, but thanks to Peter's skill at handling such things, it didn't. Of course, a couple of margaritas "on the house" helped, too. He used whatever tools he had at hand without a qualm.

He even gave himself a five-minute break in the security room, but went straight to the hidden camera over Lily's table and spent that time watching her and trying his best not to look down her dress. Damn those camera angles.

It was a quarter-to-midnight when he surrendered to the inevitable and made his way back to table number three.

And his Princess.

From the looks of things he was just in time. There was a large knight seated at the table now, dominating the game with his loud comments, his overly friendly compliments to Lily, and his massive stack of chips.

Lily was patiently trying to explain to Sir Idiot of the Thick Head that this was a table with a ten-dollar limit. And Sir Knight didn't like it one bit. "Really, sir. Ten dollars is the most I can accept." She leaned over and gently pushed the rest of the chips aside. "Have pity on your fellow players." She smiled sweetly at the man.

He responded by reaching for her bodice. Every nerve in Peter's body jumped to attention, his protective instincts rearing their heads and snarling furiously as that big paw threatened to grasp the delicate lace and embroidery covering her breasts.

Quick as lightning, Lily dodged back and shook her head at him. "No, sir. Casino rules. No touching at all." She pushed the shoe a little further onto the table. "But let's see how your luck is tonight, shall we? All bets down, everyone?"

Having diverted the drunken knight's attention away from her for the moment, Peter watched Lily puff a tiny breath through her lips, disturbing one of the little fronds of lace that brushed her mouth.

This knight could be trouble. Peter knew it down to his bones.

She needed a prince, just in case. So what if he was a frog? He was a strong frog. He was the frog equivalent of a ninja. He could bench press a large dragonfly. He would move every insect on the face of the earth to protect his princess.

He was also clearly going out of his mind, but that didn't stop Peter from moving silently through the crowd to stand next to Lily as she dealt the hand. The look she flashed him was reward enough.

Lily had obviously read the possibilities, too, and wasn't comfortable with any of them. Her eyes shone for a moment with gratitude and Peter felt his chest swell in an extraordinary way. If there'd been a convenient log at hand, he might have hopped on it and let out a "ribbit" worthy of the largest bullfrog in the swamp.

As it was, he just nodded. A bit of a let-down, but he'd hang on to his ribbits for a while – the night wasn't quite over.

Neither was the game. The knight showed a Ten of Clubs, something he was very pleased with. "Atta girl. That's my princess. I knew you'd do right by me." He licked his lips, his eyes never leaving Lily's face.

The first player went over in three cards and groaned loudly, but accepted the loss. Lily had fourteen showing and the others soon dropped out, leaving Sir Knight staring at her in eager anticipation.

"You gimme a Ace baby, and I'll take care of you but good." He tapped a finger on his chips. "I like to win."

"All in the cards, sir. I just deal them." Lily refused to look directly at him, noted Peter with approval. It was a standard technique in this kind of situation. Back off from the jerk. Don't give him any encouragement or make eye-contact unless you absolutely have to. If Peter hadn't been there, Lily's foot might well have already hit the silent alarm button to summon assistance should it be needed.

Lily pushed the final card across to the knight. It was another Ten. He grinned. "Yeah, honey. You're good." He licked his lips. "I'm gonna treat you like a princess should be treated baby. Just say the word."

He slid sideways just a little, making Peter realize he was even drunker than he'd appeared at first sight. Lifting his head, Peter saw two of the security officers mingling nearby. Thankfully, this was the sort of Casino that valued its good name and took extra care to make sure everyone had fun.

Sir Knight's idea of fun wasn't in line with the current Casino thinking. He'd be allowed to finish this hand, but with a quick movement of his head, Peter summoned security. Once the hand was done, Sir Knight was going "on crusade". *Outside* Morton's.

Lily dealt herself the final card. And, as luck would have it, she drew a Seven, giving the house the winning hand.

It wasn't really necessary for anyone to point out that the results weren't pretty. But the timing was excellent. Just as Sir Knight was about to turn belligerent, the first strokes of midnight began to chime over the loudspeakers.

The fact that one burly drunken knight was being escorted from the Casino by two even burlier men dressed as trolls attracted next to no attention at all. What did catch everybody's eye was the sudden release of thousands of glittering balloons, mixed with about a ton and a half of silver confetti.

It showered over the entire Casino floor, drenching it in a deluge of sparkling magic as everybody began to remove their masks and hoot loudly as the chimes counted down to midnight.

Lily turned to Peter, words of thanks on her lips. But he stayed them, lifting a finger to her face then untying her mask, letting it drop to the table beside them. "You okay?"

She nodded silently, watching as he untied his own, revealing that princely face she'd lost her heart to the first moment she'd set eyes on him.

"I think this is where the Princess kisses the Frog." He smiled gently as he slid an arm around her waist and pulled her snugly against him, fitting their curves, heating her with his embrace.

"And thanks him for rescuing her from the evil knight, maybe?" Lily managed a throaty whisper.

"Works for me."

And there, surrounded by the cascade of rainbows and magic, the Princess first felt the touch of her Frog Prince's lips on hers. Warm, gentle, wonderful, it was a moment that knocked every brain cell sideways in Lily's head. She tentatively moved her tongue to taste him, savoring each second until they finally parted.

"Wow." She opened her eyes, which of course she'd closed in the best tradition of Princesses getting their first kiss from their handsome Prince. "Wow."

Peter gulped and nodded. "Yeah, wow."

At this point, a real fairy-tale princess would have blushed and stammered and made some comment about the prince demanding her hand in marriage from her father, the King.

Not Lily.

She grabbed her prince and kissed him all over again. Hard.

"And so the Princess kissed the Frog, turned him into a prince, and they all lived happily ever after." Lily Macintosh closed the book and put it on the bedside table.

"Just like you and Daddy, huh?" Ryan Macintosh yawned.

"Yep. Just like me and Daddy." Lily stroked the soft hair on her son's head and tucked the blankets around him and Ribbit, his stuffed frog. "Now get some sleep. Your aunt Sarah's bringing Stephanie over to play tomorrow."

Ryan wrinkled his four-year-old nose in disdain. "She bullies me. I hate girls."

Lily chuckled. "That'll change." A sound from the doorway distracted her and she turned to see Peter grinning at them both. "Give it a few years, sweetie."

"'Kay. 'Night Mom. 'Night Daddy."

Lily rose and went to the door. "'Night darling."

"G'night spud." Peter eased the door shut behind her, looking quite wicked.

"What are you up to?" Lily whispered the words. Ryan was a sound sleeper, but still…

From behind him, Peter produced a dangling necklace that glittered in the low light of the hall. "I have something of yours, my Princess. And a set of green pajamas that are just made for a certain frog…"

Lily giggled. "I love you. And I don't have to catch flies for you either."

"You forgot to tell Ryan about my rescuing you and taking you away on my white horse." Peter led Lily to their bedroom.

"Don't rush it, okay? When he finds out my Prince's white horse is actually a Mustang…"

Peter winced. "Not just a *Mustang*, honey. A Shelby GT500. Five hundred horsepower, five-point-four liter intercooled engine, six-speed, duel exhaust…"

Lily rolled her eyes. "Whatever. It worked."

Peter held her close. "Yeah. It worked. Thank heavens for fairy tale endings, huh?"

And the moral of this little story…

Not all frogs are princes. And there's a lot of 'em out there we girls are going to have to kiss before we get to the right one with a crown.

But with a bit of magic, the chimes of midnight ringing in our ears, and the right person, all things are possible, including being swept away by a prince with a top of the line sports car.

Sometimes it isn't that hard to be green after all...

Ribbit.

The End

Sahara Kelly has written in just about every genre there is and invented a few new ones for her own amusement. You can get an idea of what she's up to at the moment by visiting her website at www.saharakelly.com

Rendezvous with Fate

*A tale of what happened after
Little Bear found Goldilocks*

Taige Crenshaw

"I told you to give me a few days before you set up any more jobs." Noelle Locke pounded the steering wheel and glared at the cell phone sitting on her coin tray before pulling onto the side road.

"I know, Noelle, but Mr. Madison was insistent that you at least come by and see his house. He's really trying to give his wife a nice anniversary gift," Kai said.

Noelle's heart softened at the thought of receiving such a romantic gift. With the luck she'd had with men, all they had ever given her was a fistful of bills and heartache. Memories best unexplored stirred. Noelle blocked them out and with a sigh and focused on the now. Kai Robbins, her best friend and business partner, knew that Noelle was a sucker for anything to do with romance.

"No, Kai. I have too much work lined up already. Why don't you do the job yourself?"

"Mr. Madison wants you. He saw the work you did on the Ammes house," Kai replied.

Noelle stifled a groan. The Ammes house was the best work she had ever done, but it hadn't been appreciated.

"Oh, *hell* no. Did you ask Mr. Madison if he'd told his wife he hired me? I don't want a repeat of what happened at the Ammes'." Noelle touched her locs, remembering the pain as Ms. Ammes jerked on her hair.

"Ms. Ammes said she was sorry, Noelle. She didn't know her husband had hired you to decorate their house as a gift. How would you have reacted if you found some strange woman in your bedroom with your husband? Putting sheets on the bed, no less. You're lucky she didn't scalp you." Kai laughed.

"She damn near did. Thank God my hair grew back. I don't find anything funny about it." Noelle pulled into the drive and snatched up the cell phone. "Why the heck doesn't Mr. Madison have a phone so I can call him?"

"He has a phone, but they're having problems with it. It wouldn't matter anyway. He and his wife left for their cruise yesterday."

"*What!* Then why the hell am I here?"

"To take a look at the house. Mr. Madison said the keys are under the front doormat, and to make yourself at home. His son bought the house for all of them to live in a few months ago, but they haven't had a chance to change the décor. You'll only be doing the bottom half of the house, since the son lives upstairs. His son is away for a few weeks, so you have the house to yourself." Kai's tone was patient.

"Are you crazy? Kai, I'm not redecorating the house with no one there to approve what I do. Heck, I didn't take the job. You did. So you do it."

"Mr. Madison already approved what he wanted. He wants the same type of feel as the Ammes house. He has signed a waiver that he will accept whatever we do."

"Pah. Like that means he or his wife won't have a fit if they don't like it. I'm not do—"

Kai cut her off. "Are you at the house?"

"Yes. It doe—"

"Have you looked at it?"

"No. It doesn't matter. I'm no—"

"Look at the house, Noelle. Then tell me 'no'." Kai's tone was smug.

"I don't see why…" Noelle turned to look at the house, and her mouth dropped open. "Oh, my God. It's like a castle."

Noelle got out and took in the mansion. The dark red brick shone in the sun. Columns and turrets covered the house. Ornate rails enclosed balconies that wrapped around the top floor. Light bounced off large bay windows. Noelle turned and looked at the immaculate gardens. A marble pathway led to the front entrance. She shook her head at the fanciful thought that at any moment, a prince might open the door to sweep her off her feet. There were no princes—at least not for her. There were only big grizzly bears of men who ate you alive if you weren't smart enough to get away.

"*Noelle.*" Kai's voice caught her attention.

"Yeah," she replied absently.

"Are you ready to get to work?" The smugness was still in her voice.

"I hate you."

"You know you love me." Kai made kissing noises.

"Like a rash on my backside." Noelle chuckled.

Kai laughed. "A rash that won't go away." Her tone went dreamy as she continued. "It's beautiful, isn't it?"

Noelle glanced at the house again, thinking it even more breathtaking than the first time she looked.

"It's all right," she replied.

"Liar. So, will you decorate it?"

"After I do the walk-through, I'll let you know."

"Okay. Call me when you're done."

Closing her phone, Noelle dropped her cell inside the pocket of her bag and closed the door of the car with her hip. As she walked up the path, she admired and smelled the flowers. She continued up the beautiful staircase to the front door, and trailed her hand along the stained glass insets. She looked closer and saw that it was various couples embracing in different loving poses.

Whoever did this is good. Really good. I'll have to ask Kai to find out who the artist is. We could use this in some of our decorating.

Noelle found the key, unlocked the door and stopped in horror.

"Ah, hell. What did they do, take a bottle of Pepto-Bismol and splash all over the room?"

Noelle continued through the various rooms, wincing at the pink on pink décor. It wasn't that she hated pink, although after today she might. The house just had too much of it.

"It's a shame what the previous owners did to this house." She reached the hallway and trailed her hand over the oak rails of the staircase leading the other second, and then glanced up. It was tempting to see if the second floor was as bad as the first. "No. I'm only to do downstairs."

At least the kitchen wasn't pink. It was high-tech and sleek. Seeing the fridge made her hungry and she opened the stainless steel door, revealing wide shelves filled with food. The shelves were filled with food.

"If the Madisons are out of town, why do they have so much food?" Her stomach growled.

As she closed the fridge she noticed a note on the door.

Welcome! I have left you food in the fridge to eat.
And I've made your favorite.
Enjoy.

The note answered her. Usually, she worked such long hours getting a house decorated that she got to know the client well, built a bond, sometimes shared meals with them. But this was the first time she'd had one leave food for her. With a shrug, she opened the fridge and looked at the contents. A covered dish caught her attention. She reached for it. "Yes! Gumbo."

She made quick work of nuking it and sat to eat. "It's too cold."

Noelle put down the spoon, took the bowl back to the microwave, and programmed it. She wandered around the kitchen and took a look outside the window, absently noting the road behind the house. The ding of the microwave caught her attention. Grabbing a dish towel, she took the bowl out and went back to the table, then pulled out a chair closer to the window and sat. The chair wobbled. She stood quickly and checked it, frowning at a cracked leg.

"Add a dining set to the list."

She tested a second chair and then sat with a wiggle. Smiling, she settled, pulled the bowl to her and took a bite.

"Hot... hhhot!" She blew out of her mouth to ease the sting.

Shaking her head, Noelle stood and left the bowl of gumbo to cool. She wandered to the door across the room, and opened it. Surprised to see a hall, she walked through the door. One by one, she opened the various rooms and saw they were all empty. The walls and curtains had the same pink-on-pink theme. The room at the end of the hall was richly decorated.

"God. Whoever had this house before sure liked pink. Oy." Stepping into the pink bedroom, she looked over the furnishings and saw that they were beautiful.

Next to the bed was a photo of a couple and a young man. They looked happy and loving. With a smile, she put the picture back down. She turned to the bed and checked the mattress, surprised by the feel. She tried it again, with the same result.

"How can anyone sleep on a bed that's as hard as rock?" Noelle heard her voice echo in the empty room. She bit her lip. "You've got to stop talking to yourself."

With a laugh, she walked around to the other side of the bed and felt it. She stood back and put her hand on her hips.

"So soft it would suck you in like a Venus flytrap. How the heck did they get a bed like this?" Noelle made a mental note to ask Kai if there was a reason for the different firmness in the bed.

Having wandered around the room and checked out every bit of it, she went back into the kitchen and took a bite of the gumbo.

"Ummm... just right." She sat and ate her meal as she thought of how she would redesign the house.

Finished, she went to the sink and cleaned out her bowl, then went back toward the front door. At the base of the staircase she looked up to the second floor.

"You're only supposed to decorate downstairs. There's no reason for you to go upstairs." Noelle glanced around and then went up the stairs.

The railing felt solidly built under her hand.

"More pink," she said as she arrived on the landing and debated which way to go. As she walked to the right, she opened doors along the way, revealing a media room, den, library, and an office. Reaching the last door, she opened it and winced.

"Oh my God."

The room was massive and covered in various shades of

pink. She had thought downstairs was as pink as it could get, but she was wrong. She closed her eyes, and then opened one to see if it was still there.

"Lots of pink. And to think, I liked pink before today."

The massive sleigh bed was in front of a floor-to-ceiling window. On the same wall was an open doorway that led to a balcony. Unable to resist, Noelle walked over to the bed, touched it, and sighed in pleasure.

"Now *that's* a bed."

The view of the field of flowers, a pond, and trees was breathtaking. She covered a yawn that escaped.

"God, I'm tired. Better leave before..." With another yawn, she took off her shoes and lay down. "Just for a minute. Then I'll go."

She looked out the window, and then fell asleep.

Pierce Madison pushed open the door, tiredness weighing on him. He dropped his bag inside the kitchen doorway. Turning, he waved at his friend Gerald, who had dropped him off. Gerald beeped his horn and turned his car around and left via the back road their houses shared. He closed the door, stepped into the kitchen, and went right to the fridge. He stopped and read the note.

"Gotta love Mom." He chuckled, remembering the call late the night before and his mom's excitement at the surprise anniversary cruise his dad had taken her on.

When he had told her he was coming home, she had wanted to cancel the trip to be there for his arrival, but he'd talked her out of it. He patted his flat stomach and laughed at his promise to his mother to eat enough. Despite her always trying to fatten him up, it wouldn't stick. He was busy traveling and was always on the go. His broad shoulders, massive chest, and height made him look intimidating. In his line of work, it was both useful and a hindrance. He brought his attention back to the note. Pierce took it down and opened the fridge, bending to search for his favorite.

"Where's the gumbo?" He looked around and saw the empty serving dish and bowl. A yawn distracted him. "I'm too tired to figure this out."

Setting the note on the counter, he walked the hall and up the stairs, yawning along the way. He walked toward his room and stopped.

"Why are all the doors open?" He thought about it, and then chuckled. "Mom was dusting again."

Shrugging, he continued down the hall to his room. He stepped inside and stopped cold at the sight before him. The woman's face was in profile away from him. Her long, dark brown hair was tinged with gold, and it was partially covering her face. Quietly, he walked around the bed and knelt on the floor next to it. Her honey skin beckoned him to touch, but he clenched his fist to resist. Her sculptured cheeks made him want to lick along her face, while her soft, kissable-looking lips made his own ache to press against hers. Stifling a groan, he looked back at her closed eyes. Her full, curling lashes fanned against her skin.

What color are your eyes?

He figured they would be chocolate brown and sexy as hell. As if she had heard his silent thoughts, her eyes opened. His breath caught, and his heart pounded against his chest. He had been right and oh so wrong.

They are sexy as hell. Out loud, he said, "Golden eyes." He leaned closer to her and looked at her beautiful eyes.

Her eyes darkened, and then her fist flew out.

"Shit!" he cried as it connected.

He got to his feet. Another blow to his chest made him stumble. She smiled, a nasty twist of the lips. Then she jumped up and swung her leg. He staggered and fell onto his butt as her foot connected with his head. He shook his head to clear the wooziness and saw a flash out of the corner of his eye. She was brandishing a lamp. With a curse, he grabbed her arm before she could connect. She fought him as he yanked the lamp out of her hand. The woman scrambled back, but he followed her and grabbed her again. She swung with her free hand. He caught it and pulled her hands behind her back, careful not to hurt her. The woman jerked her head forward, but he moved his face out of the way.

"Stop fighting me! Who the hell are you, and what are you doing sleeping in my bed?" At his words, the woman went rigid and looked at him. He was arrested by her furious golden gaze. She studied him and sighed.

"You don't look anything like the picture." There was a slightly-accented, musical cadence to her voice.

"What picture?" He watched her in confusion.

"The one in your parents' bedroom," she replied.

"What? Who the hell are you? What are you doing here?" He narrowed his gaze.

The woman returned his look. "Which one do you want me to answer first?"

He stifled a chuckle at the disgruntled tone. "Either."

"Let me go."

"Are you going to hit me again?" he asked.

"That remains to be seen." She smirked.

He let her go and she retreated, put on her shoes, and continued out the door. He followed.

"Hey! Who are you?"

He followed her as she ignored him and walked down the hall and then down the stairs. She picked up a huge purse from the entryway table. He hadn't even noticed it. She turned and faced him.

"Noelle Locke. Your father hired me to redecorate this house. It—"

"You're a decorator." Excitement filled him.

No more pink. He reached out, grabbed her, and kissed her. As his lips touched hers, his mind screamed that it was a bad idea. She stiffened, and then relaxed against him. Harsh need gripped him, and he banded his arms around her. Murmuring, he swept his tongue inside her mouth. She moaned, and her tongue dueled with his. The taste of her swept him under. It was sweet and addictive. He pulled her closer and sucked at her tongue. Noelle leaned into him and whimpered. The sound brought him to his senses.

When he withdrew and stepped back, she swayed, and he went to help her. Suddenly, she stiffened and stepped away from him. Her look was confusion, desire, and anger all mixed

together. He also glimpsed something he didn't understand—
fear.

"I'm sorry. I umm…." He searched for the words to excuse
his behavior and could find none.

The suave negotiator he was in the boardroom was useless
against the power this woman seemed to wield over him. He
took a breath and then went with his gut.

"Look, when you said you were the decorator, all I could
think of was that I wanted to kiss you if you can get me out of
living with all this pink." He gestured at the walls and ran his
hand through his hair. "Hell, that's a lie. I wanted to kiss you
when I found you sleeping in my bed. I promise not grab you
again, and I won't let a kiss like that happen again." Her
golden gaze captured him. "No. I promise not to grab you
unless you want me to. And I'll try to control myself around
you." He smiled sheepishly.

Noelle looked at him. "Does that trying to look innocent act
work on many women?"

Startled, he glanced at her and grinned. "Sometimes."

She made a rude noise, then turned and opened the door.

"Noelle, please. I'm sorry. We need you to redecorate this
house of Pepto."

"I was only hired to do the downstairs." She glanced at him
over her shoulder.

"How much to do the whole house?"

She said nothing.

"I'm sorry." Desperation filled him.

"Are you sorry you kissed me, or that I might not decorate
your house?" She watched him, her golden gaze intense.

"The house. Have you ever seen so much pink?"

Her lips twitched. "House of Pepto, indeed."

"I'm desperate. If my dad hired you to work down here, he
must trust you."

She didn't respond, but turned and went out the door. She
glanced back at him.

"Fine. I'll decorate your house. I'll be here in the morning
to go over my ideas." Noelle's voice was cool.

Pierce walked to the open door. She rummaged through

her bag and took out a pair of shades. She looked at him once more, with a small smile curving her lips.

"As for grabbing, I can't make a promise not to grab you, or to control myself." She put on her sunglasses, turned, and went down the stairs.

He watched her get in her car and drive away, then he went back inside and closed the door. As he stood in the entryway, he noticed her scent filled the area. He tried to place it.

"Almonds and vanilla," he decided. He shuddered.

He ran his hand through his hair. *How the hell am I going to control myself around her?* With a groan, he quickly went up the stairs to his room.

∾

Noelle pulled over to the side of the road and turned off the engine. She looked at her shaking hands.

"You would think you'd learned your lesson already. There are no princes, only big old grizzly bears. Grizzly bears who can kiss." At the thought of his kisses, she realized something. Her eyes widened. "I kissed him, and I don't even know his name. Way to go, Noelle."

She thumped her fist on the steering wheel.

"You can't afford to get involved with him."

∾

"Looks great, Noelle. You've done a lot in a short time."

Her body heated at the sound of his bass voice. Bracing herself, Noelle turned around and looked at Pierce Madison. Although she had been in his presence numerous times in the last week, each time she saw him, it had the same effect as the first. He captured all her senses. His face was sharp planes and angles that came together in a latent sensuality that drew her to him.

For a man so large, he moved with a gracefulness that was both startling and somehow predatory. She bit her lip, and then looked into his eyes. The pale grey of his gaze contrasted with his sun-kissed skin, deepening the intensity of his eyes. His lashes were curly and dark brown, like his hair that curled over his collar and fell in waves to the middle of his back. He raised long fingers and smoothed his hair back from his face.

Those fingers had inspired all sorts of fantasies. The thought of them touching her made her heart race and an ache fill her belly. She clenched her fist. He watched her, a bemused smile on his face. She realized she hadn't answered his question.

"Umm...yeah, thanks. It helped that my contacts were able to get everything here so fast."

"I'm just glad to see the pink go." He laughed.

She joined him. Pierce got a drink out of the fridge and closed it. Coming closer to where she sat on the newly-installed island, he leaned against it.

"I've been meaning to ask you something." Pierce hesitated. "My folks will be back in a little over three weeks. I want to throw them an anniversary party a few days after they get back, but I'm having trouble finding a party planner at this late date. I know you're an interior designer, but do you, by any chance, know any party planners?"

Noelle opened her mouth to say 'no', but couldn't at the earnest expression on his face. "Yes, I do."

"Great. Do you think they could plan the party for me?"

"I don't know. Let me make a call."

"Thanks, Noelle," Pierce said, then went back out the kitchen door.

Sighing, Noelle wondered what Julianne would ask in return for the favor she was about to request. She called her.

"Hey, Jules. I need a favor. I have a client who is planning a party for his parents' anniversary in approximately four weeks."

There was silence on the other end of the phone.

"Jules, are you there?"

"I'm trying to place the voice. It sounds distantly familiar."

She chuckled. "Come on, Jules. You know who it is."

"I would if you would at least return a call."

"Are you done yet?"

"Nah. Just getting around to the part about you remembering you have a sister. Even though you live in your own place behind the main house on the family property, I barely see you."

"I know I have a sister. I've been busy." Noelle chuckled.

"So busy you missed our last family movie night?" Julianne asked .

Noelle winced at the reproach in her tone. "I know. I'm sorry. I have to get this job done in a short space of time. Pierce wants—"

"Pierce? Who is this Pierce?"

"Umm… the client I mentioned. The one who needs an anniversary party planned for his parents in about four weeks."

"Yeah, right. This is your big sis. Who is this man that makes you sound like that when you say his name?"

Noelle bit back a curse. She knew she was in for a grilling if she wasn't careful.

"No one. Just a client. Can you fit him in?"

Julianne finally said, "Sure. I'll meet with him and squeeze him in. Send him by tomorrow at 10 a.m."

Noelle knew it wasn't as easy as Julianne made it sound. Julianne was the most sought after party planner in Singleton, New York, and was booked for months in advance. Heck, Julianne was sought after all over the state. For her to fit Pierce in would take a lot of maneuvering.

"What's it going to cost me?" Noelle asked, afraid to know.

"I'll let you know at a later date. 'Bye."

Noelle hung up and went to look for Pierce. Going into the living room, she saw he was relaxing on the couch. She stood in the doorway and watched him. As if feeling her gaze on him, he turned to her.

"You have a meeting with a party planner tomorrow at 10 a.m.," she said.

Pierce stood, a smile on his face, and started toward her.

"Whoa. That's what got you in trouble last time. A 'thanks' is enough." Noelle turned to walk away.

His hard hands grabbed her and turned her back around. The hunger in his eyes made her breath stall. Pierce's gaze trailed over her like a physical touch. Then he met her gaze.

"How long are we going to skirt around these feelings?" Pierce's voice was soft.

"I don't—"

"Tsk, Noelle. Don't lie. Admit it, or say nothing."

"Fine. You want the truth? I want you with an ache that borders on pain." She watched the need flash on his face as he reached for her. She stepped out of the way.

"No, Pierce. I don't do casual sex. Not anymore. It leaves me cold, and I've been hurt too often." She turned and walked away.

"This isn't casual." His quiet words stopped her.

"What do you mean?" She turned to look at him.

"How do you tell a woman you only met a few days ago you want more? Hell, a woman you haven't done anything with except kiss, once. How do you tell her you ache to have her, and need to be around her, despite her prickly nature?" Pierce's smile was teasing, then bittersweet. "How can you say you love someone who makes you feel vulnerable, and yet still like a man?"

Noelle's heart pounded, and tears filled her eyes. "You can't love me. We only just met."

Pierce smiled tenderly and walked over to her.

"I started to fall here." A touch on her forehead. "Then ache here." With a soft touch of his fingers over her eyes. "Desire you here." Then he ran his finger over her lips. "Then I loved you for what you are here." He placed his hand over her heart. "I love all those parts of you, Noelle." She could read the truth in his eyes .

Noelle shivered with fear and desire. . With a breath, she took a chance.

"I can't say I love you. At least not yet. But this isn't casual for me, either." She cupped his face and kissed him. It was a hungry clash of tongues. She pulled back. "Pierce, *please.*" His smile was darkly sensual. He lifted her and kissed her. Noelle's heart raced, and heat pooled in her stomach from the mastery of his kiss. He carried her up the stairs, down the hall, and into his bedroom, laying her on the bed, then stepped back to undress. Noelle shifted and waited for him to join her.

"What are you doing out here?" Noelle's voice was soft.

Pierce enjoyed hearing her speak with that slightly musical cadence. Noelle had told him she was born in St. Thomas and moved to Singleton with her family when she about ten years. She padded over to him on bare feet. When she reached him, he pulled her into his arms and settled her back against his chest. She sighed and leaned against him, filling him with contentment. It was times like these he enjoyed the most. Mornings spent together cuddling or talking. Although they had only been lovers for almost two weeks, he felt as if he had been waking up with her forever. She looked back at him. He kissed her soft lips, and then pulled away.

"Watching the sun rise with you, Golden Eyes," he replied to the question she had asked.

Noelle grinned. "Sounds good."

They watched the sunrise together, and then got ready for the day.

An hour later, he walked into the kitchen and stopped. Noelle stood in front of the large bay windows next to the table. He continued over to her, hugging her from behind. Her breath hitched, and her body trembled. Pierce chuckled and wrapped his arms around her, placing his palms over her stomach. Noelle sighed and leaned back against him, and then turned her head and kissed him on the chin. He glanced at her lovely face. He kissed her lips softly, and then looked outside.

"Don't forget, we have reservations at six." He tried to contain his excitement.

"Don't worry. I'll be here." Noelle glanced at him. "That's the seventh time you've reminded me since we got up. Why are you so anxious?"

He changed the subject. "What have you got planned today?"

Noelle gave him a look that clearly said she knew what he was trying to do, but let it go as she replied. "Since I finished your house, I'm starting a new project."

"Did I tell you thanks for saving me from the Pepto House?"

"Many, many times." Noelle laughed.

"Well, thanks again."

"You're welcome. What are you doing today?"

"First I have to meet with Julianne to finalize the details for the party. Thanks for that, too."

"Say it like you mean it." She pursed her lips.

He chuckled. "Your sister is a perfectionist, and demanding. I've told her she can go ahead and do what she thinks is best, but she still insists on meetings to discuss details."

Noelle bit her lip.

"I sounded pitiful, didn't I?" he asked.

Noelle nodded. "Oh, yes. And that pout was priceless."

"I don't pout." He glanced at the glass and saw that he was. He sighed. "You can laugh at me all you want, but it's just an excuse to grill me about you."

"If you're looking for sympathy, you're out of luck. I told you what to tell her."

He thought she was crazy and looked at her. Noelle looked serious.

"I can't tell your sister—how did you put it? Ah, yes. 'Mind your own business, Julianne, or Noelle is going to sic your mom on you.' How does that sound?"

Noelle shrugged. "If you had, she wouldn't be still teasing you about us."

"Teasing? Is that what you call it?"

"She likes you." Noelle patted his cheek.

"She does?" He was surprised.

"Yeah. If she didn't, she would never have planned your party, or insisted on these meetings."

He looked at her suspiciously. "You know something. What did she say?"

Noelle stepped out of his loosened hold and went to her bag on the island. She pulled it onto her shoulder and looked at him.

"Jules enjoys the look you get on your face."

"What look?" He narrowed his eyes.

Noelle laughed and left the room. He followed her and touched her arm. She turned to face him, a devilish look in her eye.

"She calls it your 'so befuddled in love you can't help but grin like an idiot face'. Jules has a weird sense of humor." Noelle rolled her eyes and grinned. She wandered over to the front door and touched the stained glass. "I still have to see your workshop."

"You keep distracting me," he interjected.

"It's all mutual." Noelle blew him a kiss.

"I can't believe you made this." She shook her head. "A suave businessman." She walked over to him and touched his face. "Sexy and scrumptious." Then squeezed his butt and laughed, then went back to the door. "And an artist. You really are talented." Touching one finger along the glass.

"Marry me, Noelle." As the words slipped out, Pierce cursed silently.

He hadn't meant to ask her this way. He had it all planned—wine and dine her, then propose under the stars on the balcony.

"I love you, Noelle. Marry me." He stepped closer to her.

Noelle stiffened, flinching as she had done every time he had said 'I love you' since the first. She turned to him, her eyes bleak.

"We barely know each other. You'll lea—"

"Don't say it," he warned as hurt filled him. "What do I have to say or do to make you believe me?"

"Nothing. I know you think you —"

He interrupted her. "I'm tired of trying to prove my love to you. What do you want, Noelle?. A guarantee I won't betray you? It's not going to happen. Love has no guarantee. You either accept it or not."

He stepped closer to her and ignored Noelle's instinctive step back. Pierce crowded her against the door, putting a hand on each side of her head, caging her. Her breathing was harsh as she stared down. After a few moments, she lifted her chin defiantly.

"Love has no expiration date, Noelle. I'm not all those bullshit men who hurt you. I'm Pierce, the man who loves you and wants to marry you."

She flinched after each word. With a bitter laugh, he

stepped back.

"I'm the man who refuses to stifle how I feel in fear that you will cringe like I'm about to hurt you." He clenched his fist and pounded it on his chest. "I'm Pierce, and I refuse to pay for the crimes of all those other men who hurt you." He took a breath and continued softly. "You've made a point of never once saying I love you, Noelle. You never put yourself out there. "

Her look was startled.

"Yes, I've noticed. But I thought I felt it in your touch. Was I wrong?"

Silence. Hurt cut off his breath. He turned away, unable to watch her.

"Pierce, I'm sorry." Noelle's voice was choked, and she put her hand on his arm .

He shrugged her off. "Just go, Noelle."

He heard her leave. Pierce put his hand over his heart. In a fast move, he turned, picked up a vase on the table next to the door, and flung it into the wall. He dropped to his knees.

"Noelle." Tears burned his eyes as he dropped his head and wept bitterly.

Hearing a crash, Noelle reached for the door. She stopped before opening it. She put her hand over her mouth to stop any sound from escaping and rushed down the stairs. Reaching her car, she got in, turned on the engine, and sped down the road. Tears blurred her vision, until she couldn't see to drive to see to drive. Hiccupping, she pulled over and dropped her head on the steering wheel. Agony coated her, but she couldn't give Pierce what he wanted. Letting him believe she was resistant to love only because of the men who had hurt her was easier than admitting the truth. She had promised herself long ago that she would not be vulnerable again.

Thoughts best forgotten crowded her mind. Sitting back, she put her hand over her stomach. Her womb clenched. She raised a shaky hand and pushed back her hair.

"Oh, God. I've already lost one man I love and our child. I couldn't bear for it to happen again." She wiped her eyes. "I won't let it happen. Pull it together, Noelle."

She put the car in gear and continued on.

"Noelle, you're a fool," a languid voice said.

"She is not a fool," another defended.

"Thanks, Kai. I'm glad you've come around to my side." Noelle glanced at her and then pointedly at her sister.

"Don't give me that nasty look," Julianne responded.

"I don't think you're a fool," Kai said. "I think you're a blooming idiot to let that man go." She shook her head.

Noelle groaned and dropped her head back on her couch. After leaving Pierce's house, she had known she couldn't work, so she had canceled all her appointments and holed up in her house, hoping her large extended family and friends would leave her alone to deal with this as she wanted. She should have known better—in two days they'd descended on her. At least Julianne and Kai had convinced the rest of the family to leave her be. But Julianne and Kai had refused to leave, and when they weren't at work, they hadn't given her a moment alone. They had moved in.

"I don't want to talk about it. Don't you all have to go to work or something?"

Julianne and Kai exchanged a look that made her uneasy. Kai sat back and said nothing.

"What are you afraid of, Noelle?" Julianne's look was serious.

They had badgered her relentlessly, screamed and cursed at her. All that she could handle, but this question evoked too many emotions. She closed her eyes and said nothing. Julianne grabbed her hand and sat next to her. Kai sat on the other side and took her other hand. The expression on their faces let Noelle know they would not accept a false answer.

She pulled away from them and stood. "I can't." They opened their mouths to interrupt, but Noelle kept talking. "No. Look guys, I know you mean well. But this is none of your business."

Julianne's eyes narrowed, and Kai got a stubborn look on her face. Kai grabbed her bag, while Julianne took up her briefcase. Kai opened the door, but Julianne looked back at Noelle.

"Ask yourself this, Noelle. By keeping your heart buried, you lost yourself a good man. And for what? Because you're afraid of being hurt?" Julianne closed her eyes, and when they opened, the pain in them made Noelle's breath catch. "We've all been hurt in different ways, Noelle—hurt so bad it felt as if you wanted to die. But we lived. We survived." She could hear the tears in Julianne's voice before she cleared her throat and continued. "When are you going to start living?"

Julianne took out her shades, put them on, and went out the door, passing Kai. Kai gave Noelle a look etched with her own private pain, then followed behind Julianne, closing the door behind her. Noelle collapsed on the couch, crying. She covered her mouth with her hand. Leaning her head back against the couch, she thought of what Julianne had said.

"You might be right, Julianne, but it's too painful to open yourself." Slowly, she stood and went into her bedroom.

She sat on the side of bed and opened the nightstand drawer. Taking out a picture, she traced the image there. The lines of his face that usually, even after all this time, made her heart pound didn't have the same effect. She lay in the bed, clutched the picture to her chest and rocked.

"Michael, I can't be vulnerable like that again."

Let me go, Noelle. His voice seemed to echo through her soul.

She shuddered and closed her eyes. A touch seemed to flit across her face. She turned into it, and then the feeling was gone. With purpose, Noelle sat up and put the photo back in the drawer. She kissed her fingers and touched the drawer.

"Goodbye, Michael."

She stood, grabbing her bag on the way to the door. Half an hour later, Noelle opened the door to Pierce's house and stepped inside. Quickly, she headed for the staircase.

"You must be Noelle," a female voice said.

She stiffened and looked back. Bemused, Noelle warily watched the woman coming toward her. The woman engulfed her in a hug before she could say a word. She didn't pull away.

The woman's eyes told Noelle who she was.

"Clarissa, let the young woman go," a gruff voice said.

"She's fine, Jackson." The woman laughed and stepped back.

The man walked up to join her. Clarissa leaned against her husband, who stood behind her.

The woman spoke. "Now, young woman, I hope you're here to fix the hurt you've made to my Little Bear."

"Little Bear?" Noelle asked.

"Pierce. He hates when I call him that, but he'll always be my Little Bear." The woman smiled sheepishly, and then looked serious. "Please tell me you're here to see him."

Noelle gulped at the intensity of her grey eyed gaze, so much like Pierce's. *What a way to meet his parents.*

"Umm… yes ma'am. I'm here to see Pierce."

"What are you waiting for? Go on." Clarissa made a shooing motion of her hand.

"Rissa, stop pushing the young lady," Jackson said as he gave Clarissa an indulgent look. Then he looked at Noelle. "Don't hurt our son anymore."

Guilt filled Noelle but there was nothing she could say in response.

He turned and pulled his wife with him. She stopped and looked at Noelle.

"Is your sister married?" Clarissa asked.

"No."

Clarissa smiled. "Good. We'll introduce her to Gerald."

"Rissa, no matchmaking," Jackson admonished.

She patted his hand. "It's only an introduction." Clarissa looked back at Noelle. "Now go on, dear, while we finish our meeting with your sister."

"Umm… you're back earlier than planned."

"After this lunkhead admitted he'd had the house decorated, and after I spoke with Little Bear, I knew we had to come home. They couldn't keep me away." Clarissa chuckled. "Come on, Jackson. Let's finalize this party, then go out to sit on the porch."

Clarissa went back into the living room, where Julianne sat

in one of the chairs. Julianne nodded, and then said something to Clarissa she was too far away to hear. Noelle looked back at Pierce's father.

"He's in his bedroom." He smiled and gestured up the stairs.

Noelle turned and walked up the stairs, to the right of the hall to Pierce's room. She took a breath and opened the door to see he was on the bed.

"Mom, I'll be down in a while to eat the gumbo you made," Pierce said, without looking around.

"Pierce."

He stiffened and said nothing. She went around the bed and knelt. His eyes were cool, his face expressionless. The words she had practiced all the way here stuck in her throat. Instead, she went with instinct.

"I was attracted from here." She touched his forehead. "Then I was captured from here." She feathered her hand over his eyes. "The need came from here." She ran her finger over his lips. "My admiration was already born from the way you are here." She placed her hand over his heart. "I care about all these parts of you, Pierce." She paused. "All these parts loved me despite my being unable to say it in return. I need to tell you about a man I loved named Michael."

She sat back and didn't look at him as she continued. "I met Michael seven years ago. He was debonair, loving, and treated me like a queen. I treated him as my king. We fell in love and decided to get married. We were in the middle of planning our wedding when I found out I was pregnant. Michael was ecstatic and wanted to get married right away. I was happy about the baby, but I had my dream of what I wanted for our wedding. It had all been planned already. So I convinced him to wait. Convinced him we had all the time in the world. I was wrong." She paused.

"We were on our way home from my sister's house. It was late and snowing lightly, but icy. We hit a patch of ice and slammed into a guard rail. I was ejected from the car, and when I came to, I tried to get to Michael. God, I tried. He was unconscious inside the car. I was steps away from the car when it exploded. The force threw me again, and I blacked out. When I woke, they told me Michael was dead and that I had lost my baby. It hurt. Oh, it hurt. I wanted to die, but my family and friends wouldn't let me. For a long time, I blamed myself, then Michael. Then both of us. When I finally stopped placing blame, I vowed never to love like that again, never to open myself to that sort of pain. I've dated a bunch of losers—men who I knew were not anyone I would want to marry, users who weren't looking for love. I didn't realize I was still punishing myself for being alive when Michael and my baby were dead."

She wiped her tears away. "When I met you, I had just broken up with another loser. I let you think that was what held me back, but it wasn't. I knew you were different. I knew that you would demand more than I could give. But I couldn't let myself be without you."

Noelle took a deep breath and finally looked at him. The tears on his face made her heart soften.

"It wasn't until I met you that I let someone in again." She came up on her knees and placed her hand over his heart. "It wasn't until you that I wanted to truly live." Noelle looked him in the eye. "I love you, Pierce Madison. I love you with every fiber of my soul."

Pierce sat up and pulled her into his arms. He hugged her tightly and rained kisses along her face.

"I love you, Noelle."

The words washed over her, bathing her with joy. She gripped him and kissed him, and he kissed back, their tongues tangled together. He turned and put her back on the bed. It brought her to her senses.

"Wait. Your parents are downstairs."

Pierce groaned and lay back on the bed next to her. She reached out to touch him.

"Gimme a minute," Pierce said.

She waited. After a few moments, he sighed and stood. He pulled her up in his arms. Noelle laid her hand over his heart. The steady beat of it was comforting.

"Will you marry me, Pierce?"

"What? No getting on one knee? Where's my engagement ring?" He smiled.

She smacked his chest. He gripped her hand and kissed her fingers.

"Golden Eyes, from the first moment I found you asleep in my bed, I knew you would be mine. Yes, I'll marry you."

Pierce let her go, opened his night stand, and took out a box. He took out a ring, and holding her hand in his, he put the ring on her finger.

"Next time, if you're going to propose, come prepared. I'll lend you this, since you don't have one for me."

Noelle looked at the diamond and ruby engagement ring, then at him.

"You are so not getting this back. It's mine now." She pulled him to her and kissed him hard. "And Little Bear, there won't be any other proposal for us."

"Crap. Mom told you." Pierce winced.

She chuckled. "Yes. Now let's go have some gumbo."

"You've slept in my bed, eaten my gumbo, and broken my chair. You're my very own Goldie Locke." Pierce grinned.

"Cheesy. So cheesy." Noelle laughed.

"I know. But this time, you're not getting to the gumbo and eating it all." He pushed her hand away and ran for the door. Laughing, Noelle raced through the door after him. Pierce caught her and spun her around.

"I love you, Golden Eyes," he said as he lowered his head.

"I love you, my Bear."

Pierce laughed. Noelle curled her hands around his head and kissed him.

The End

Taige Crenshaw has been enthralled with the written word from the time she picked up her first book. It wasn't long before she started to make up her own tales of romance.

Her novels are set in the modern day between people who know what they want and how to get it. Taige also sets her stories in the future with vast universes between beautiful, strange and unique beings with lots of spice and sensuality added to her work.

Always hard at work creating new and exciting places, Taige can be found curled up with a hot novel with exciting characters when she is not creating her own. Join her in the fun and frolic, with interesting people and far reaches of the world in her novels.

Website: http://www.taigecrenshaw.com

Email: http://www.taigecrenshaw.com/contact.shtml

Sleeping Beauty

Vijaya Schartz

Kyle Dormant awoke to a loud ringing. Not the alarm clock, but a sustained keening that filled his ears and vibrated through his entire body. Gasping for air, he attempted to move but couldn't. Not another episode! He knew he wasn't asleep or dreaming. He could clearly see the familiar bedroom, the dark posts of the canopy bed and the sapphire velvet drapes.

Despite the fear that gripped him, Kyle tried to relax and surrender to the paralysis that claimed his body. No point in panicking. This would pass. As his breathing eased, his fear lessened, but he still couldn't move.

Kyle sensed an invisible presence in the room. Was he losing his mind? Then the bedroom blurred, and vivid images rushed toward him, like the accelerated newsreel of an old TV broadcast. Kyle stared, helpless.

The face of a beautiful woman filled the screen, flashing on and off. Blond hair tightly knotted in a bun, she wore a white coat and clear protective eyewear that didn't detract from her stunning blue eyes. She had a kind smile. He could see her lips move, but the words were lost in the keening vibration.

The high-pitched sound faded and the images vanished. The paralysis subsided. Kyle could see his bedroom once again. Hesitantly, he moved one toe, one arm, and then tossed up the sheets, unsettling the Siamese cat sleeping on the bed.

"Sorry, Tasha." Kyle stepped onto the Persian silk rug, perfectly fine, alert, and limber. He'd had such episodes before but had no idea what they meant.

In need of serenity, he slipped on his sweats and stepped

into the greenhouse to water the rare orchids. They had been his mother's and after her early passing from breast cancer, Kyle had assumed responsibility for them. He just couldn't let the fragile plants die. He'd convinced himself that as long as the orchids thrived, his mother's spirit remained around him.

Kyle fed Tasha and then stopped by the study and opened his laptop. How did one research strange episodes like the one he had just experienced? He Googled "temporary paralysis upon awakening."

"Wow!" Apparently, Kyle wasn't alone. Hundreds of sites offered information about sleep disorders, including one called Sleep Paralysis. When he clicked on the link, the lovely face he'd seen in his hallucination popped up. Her blond hair fell below her shoulders and she didn't wear plastic goggles, but there was no mistaking the striking blue eyes or the kind smile.

Dr. Talia Beauregard, sleep disorder specialist, conducted studies on Sleep Paralysis, an affliction with the very symptoms of Kyle's episode. His vision of her could not be a coincidence.

Somewhat reassured that his ordeal was benign, Kyle wondered why he'd seen Dr. Beauregard's face in his hallucination. Talia...a pretty name for a gorgeous woman. Her clinic was a few blocks down the street. On impulse, Kyle filled the online application to participate in her study.

Then he went for his morning jog.

Half-way to the park, his cell phone chimed, and he flipped it open without slowing down. "Kyle," he announced, somewhat winded, expecting his father with a reminder about the board meeting.

"This is Dr. Talia Beauregard." The voice sounded as kind, smart, and congenial as the picture. "You volunteered for my sleep study from the site. Can we save some time and meet before work?"

Kyle slowed to a halt, catching his breath. "You mean now?" He checked his Rolex. He had ample time before the board meeting. "You drink coffee?"

"Sure."

He remembered her office was not far. "Starbucks on the

corner of Hayden and Happy Valley Roads, in twenty minutes?"

"Perfect."

Kyle flipped the phone, his heart beating faster than if he'd run a marathon. Just enough time to jog there.

"Hot Chai, please." Talia watched the barista prepare her order. She'd lied. She didn't drink coffee. But she felt lucky. This prospective subject seemed to offer the perfect profile for her research. A respected member of the upper class, only heir to the Dormant fortune. His family owned a large road construction company. Nothing strange or New Age about this serious, young man.

Talia had seen her share of weirdos. What people went through during sleep paralysis made them believe they had a spiritual experience. Some even thought they had been abducted by aliens.

As a scientist, Talia understood the anomaly. Dream state paralysis was a natural safety measure, to prevent the sleepers from acting up their dreams. In the affected subjects, the mind awoke from sleep while the body remained under the paralysis of dream state for a few minutes longer. Nothing alien about it, and she intended to prove it once and for all.

Chai in one hand, briefcase in the other, she picked a table by the window and sat, watching each incoming young male, looking for Kyle Dormant.

"Dr. Beauregard?" The deep melodic voice came from behind her.

Startled, Talia turned to face the man. "Mr. Dormant?" The gray Ralph Lauren jogging sweats took her by surprise. Somehow, she'd expected a suit, like on his company's website, not the debonair smile of an athlete, tanned, flushed, with a sheen of perspiration.

"Please, call me Kyle." He pulled up the chair and sat facing her. A rebellious lock of black hair fell over a wide brow. His deep brown eyes sparkled with feral interest. Nothing like his stiff portrait.

"All right, Kyle."

"So... I'm all yours. What do you want to know?"

Somehow the words brought heat to Talia's cheeks. She had to remind herself to stick to the study.

"Well, your profile looks good." She glanced at him sideways... boy did it ever. Instinctively, she checked his left hand, satisfied no wedding band adorned his ring finger. "But I need to ascertain that you are right for this study. When did you have your last experience?"

"This morning." His direct stare increased her embarrassment. He certainly had no problems with self-confidence. His hand on the table almost touched hers.

Talia shivered, wondering how his hands would feel on her body... Not that she would ever mix business with pleasure. It would be highly unethical to pursue a relationship with one of her study subjects. She could lose her objectivity and her hard-earned reputation in the medical field as a serious scientist.

She opened her leather case to give herself countenance and pulled out a questionnaire and her silver Tiffany pen. "How do you feel about answering a bunch of very personal questions and sleeping in front of a camera, with instruments monitoring your brain activity?"

"Fine with me." He grinned. "As long as it doesn't interfere with my work during the day, and doesn't involve needles."

Talia chuckled. Amazing how so many grown men feared needles. "No needles. I promise."

Two hours later, Kyle sat in the conference room of D&D Road Engineering and observed the board members, most of them in Armani suits, most of them family members. For once, they all attended. Kyle's father sat at the end of the table and glanced nervously at the door. Why? Five past ten, and his father always started on time.

A commotion and rapid footsteps in the hallway silenced the chatting businessmen. A man in rumpled khakis with unkempt gray hair rushed in, followed by two flustered security guards.

A general gasp went around the table at the sight of this unshaved character.

"Sorry, sir," a security guard muttered to Kyle's father. "We could not stop him."

"That's all right, Ricardo." The CEO waved a dismissing hand. "I was expecting him."

Ricardo's eyes widened, but he nodded and motioned to the other guard to follow him out of the room.

Kyle's father turned to the rumpled newcomer. "It's about time!" he exclaimed with surprising petulance.

When the man took the seat next to Kyle's father, the one that always remained empty, Kyle realized who he was. Despite the disheveled state, the resemblance became striking. Uncle Gerald!

The two brothers had started the company in their early years but Gerald had soon lost interest and went abroad, happily spending the money Kyle's father made for him. So, why had he returned from his exotic travels after all these years?

Kyle's father rose and buttoned his jacket.

The room quieted.

"I made an important decision." His solemn tone confirmed the gravity of his words. "I am retiring from active management. I leave this company with all my shares in Kyle's capable hands. This shouldn't come as a surprise. I have been grooming him for years…"

Stunned, Kyle missed the next few sentences. He had no clue this was coming.

"I wish this company and all of you the best of luck." His father checked his watch. "And now, if you'll excuse me, I have an urgent tee time to make at the Princess Golf Resort." Without another word, Kyle's father turned on his heel and left the room with a happy spring in his step.

After the door closed, a murmur rose and grew into a crescendo.

Kyle banged his fist on the table. "Silence!" he shouted over the cacophony of voices. "We have a lot to go through." As the youngest member, now in charge, he had to regain control of the room. "The main topic of this meeting is to decide on whether or not to bid on the government contract for the loop 505."

"Work for the government and you'll go broke before you get paid." Uncle Gerald railed, staring at Kyle with defiance.

"This contract is a sure thing." Kyle struggled to keep his voice calm. "It will secure the future of the company and provide much needed job security for our employees for years to come. It's important to them in these uncertain times."

Uncle Gerald snorted. "You have it all wrong, kid. I say we should bid for smaller, private corporation deals such as shopping centers. That's where the money is. Short term, quick pay, private funds. It's much more profitable."

"Where have you been for the past two years?" Kyle had to keep the trust of the other investors and family members. "The private sector has crumbled in the stock market crash. No one builds shopping centers these days. "

Cries of agreement and dissention rose; comments ensued. The tone rose a few decibels, and soon everyone shouted at the same time, and no one was heard. Why had his father dropped this bomb without warning?

Banging his gavel, Kyle obtained relative order for the rest of the meeting, which ended in a deadlock. The board scheduled another session for the next day. Kyle wondered how his father kept control of this noisy bunch of relatives. Although he was grateful for the opportunity to lead, Kyle didn't feel quite ready for the task.

Back in his office after the meeting, he heard a knock on the door.

"Come in, it's open." Kyle expected his assistant.

When his Uncle Gerald walked in, Kyle struggled to control his anger.

Gerald offered a meek, apologetic smile. "Sorry, kid. Nothing personal." He dragged a backpack that seemed out of place. "Although I'm not here much, I do care about what happens to this company. It's my baby, too."

Kyle felt a tinge of guilt, although he couldn't tell why. "Conflict can be constructive. Your arguments have value. I will consider them carefully. Maybe we can bid on mid-size government jobs and take on diversified private contracts as well."

Gerald's smile widened. "Don't worry, kid. All will be fine. And to prove it to you, I brought you something for your collection. She's a beauty."

Out of the backpack, with infinite care, Gerald pulled an elongated plastic globe clouded by condensation.

Kyle had to refrain from showing his excitement. "Is it what I think it is?"

Gerald carefully handed the globe to Kyle. "An orchid so rare, it hasn't been catalogued yet. A splendid specimen. The locals call it Sleeping Beauty."

Kyle took the clear globe with reverence. "Strange name. Any particular reason?"

"I guess it sleeps for years before blooming. I wouldn't open it until you get into your greenhouse, however. Very fragile, I'm told."

Kyle could barely see the delicate white flower through the fogged plastic, but he knew better than to open such a sensitive plant to the dry atmosphere of an air-conditioned office. He couldn't wait to get to the greenhouse and uncover this unique orchid. Maybe Uncle Gerald wasn't so bad after all. "I don't know how to thank you. Where did you find it?"

"Bhutan. They grow wild over there, but they're not easy to find. You wouldn't believe what I went through to get it. Not including my battle with agricultural inspection to bring it into the US. Good thing I know a few people in high places. The smile on your face makes it all worthwhile."

Still, Kyle had to be frank. "Why are you so considerate in private, when you fought me tooth and nail, and made me look like a fool in front of the board?"

Gerald frowned at Kyle's directness.

Kyle wondered why Gerald had gone away. Did he feel uncomfortable among the other siblings? Or, had they pushed him away? They rarely spoke of him, and always in hushed voices. Gerald was taboo. For Kyle, the man remained a mystery, and as such, fascinating.

Gerald sighed. "I guess your father never told you."

"Told me what?" Kyle realized he knew nothing about his

uncle.

"About your mother." Genuine sadness misted the man's eyes, and his voice choked. "You see... your mother and I met at your parents' wedding and decided that for your father's sake, we should never be in the same room alone." He chuckled dryly. "Or better yet, not in the same country."

Kyle found it difficult to believe that his mother had a secret love for this man, but he went along. "So that's why you disappeared and spent your dividends instead of joining the company?" Every family had its skeletons, and Kyle had just discovered one. "Why didn't you come back after Mother died?"

"I would have been a thorn in your father's side. By then he was used to ruling the company alone. And he did it well."

But Gerald was back now, and wanted to manage the company himself. Kyle could not erase the gut feeling that he had come back to take over. "Is this a bribe? I will not give up my chair."

"I don't expect you to." The older man didn't fight back, probably out of consideration for Kyle's dead mother. He just smiled and waved as he walked out the door.

Back at the Scottsdale Tuscan villa, Kyle took his precious gift to the greenhouse and selected a spot where the light would be kind to the plant. He set the globe in a prominent place among the other orchids. Then, delicately, he removed the clear plastic dome. What a gorgeous flower! Mainly white, it had wide delicate petals reminiscent of a butterfly, with a scalloped edge. The pink heart formed a smooth pouch with tiger spots. Force of habit, Kyle caressed the underside of the flower's heart.

"Ouch!" He winced at the painful prick.

Of all things! The flower had a hidden thorn. Although Kyle had never heard of thorns on an orchid, he knew many species hadn't been discovered yet, and the possibilities were infinite, mainly among the wild varieties. He sucked the blood off his fingertip and found the taste reminiscent of licorice.

Satisfied with the position of the new orchid in his green

house, Kyle ate, wrote in his journal, fed Tasha, then took a shower and changed into casual sweats. He had to meet Dr. Talia Beauregard at the clinic down the street for his first night of sleep study.

Facing Kyle across the glass desk, Talia found it difficult to remain professional. As she went through the usual briefing, her mind wandered into forbidden territory. She imagined Kyle's toned body naked under the designer sweats. He looked like a Ralph Lauren model and smelled of expensive cologne. From the stylish hair to the Air Jordans, everything about him screamed refinement and taste. Yet he answered the most personal questions with a candor that would make even a physician blush. How did he do that?

Another question, not on the form, burned Talia's lips. She had to know. This man looked too good to be true. "Are you gay?"

Kyle's brown eyes softened. "If I were gay, I wouldn't be here tonight." His deep voice seemed to caress her. "I have to confess that when I saw your portrait on the website, I did a double take. I recognized your face from my vision during this morning's episode. It could be a sign." He flashed a devilish grin. "Perhaps we are destined for each other."

"I don't believe in destiny." Not another weirdo! Despite the fact that she could barely control her hormones in his presence, Talia refused to have anything to do with daydreamers. "I hope you are not making things up."

Kyle shook his head. "Not my style."

"I need my men to be solidly anchored in reality." It didn't sound right.

"Are you speaking about the study?" Still grinning, he covered her hand with his.

Talia's skin tingled with unfamiliar tendrils of electricity that traveled up her arms.

He seemed to enjoy her surprise. "For a second, there, it almost sounded as if you were talking about your private life."

"My taste in men applies to both work and play." Her bold reply surprised Talia. What was it about him? Reluctantly she pulled away her hand. "But I could never have a relationship with a patient."

"Oh, a patient. Of course." Kyle settled back in his chair, his expression serious, unreadable. "That's good. You see, the company takes most of my time. I don't have the luxury of nurturing relationships. Too many responsibilities, I guess."

"That could be your excuse for not trying. Relationships take work." Talia smiled, glad to have regained control of the conversation. "Relationships can also influence your sleeping pattern. Do you have anyone special at the moment?"

"Just Tasha."

"Tasha?" Talia struggled to hide her disappointment behind a neutral tone.

Kyle chuckled. "She is Siamese and very affectionate." He grinned as if he knew she could be jealous.

"Tasha is a cat?" Excitement bubbled inside her, but Talia maintained a calm demeanor. Why did she feel like a college girl in front of this man?

"By the way, your comment could apply to you as well." Kyle winked. "Maybe you are using professionalism as an excuse for not dating. Although in your case it might be more about fear of being known than reluctance to make it work."

Talia braced herself. Was she that transparent? "Sorry about the personal remarks. I think we should keep this conversation on a professional level." Talia rose from her chair.

He stood up, like a perfect gentleman.

"If you would follow me to your bedroom." She flushed at the lusty images her words had just conjured.

Amusement danced in Kyle's eyes as he picked up his Louis Vuitton gym bag and followed her out of the office into the clinic hallway. Obviously, the irony wasn't lost on him. Talia's second Freudian slip today.

After opening the door, Talia turned on the light. A battery of electronic instruments sat on a wall shelf. Instead of a headboard, a large open hood of clear plastic loomed like a half canopy above the head of the bed. To the side, a functional table and chair completed the decor.

Talia went to the window, which offered a moonlit scene of

saguaro-studded mountains, and closed the linen drapes. "There is a full bathroom. If you need to get up during the night, go right ahead. Just don't knock your head on the hood."

"No needles, right?" Kyle dropped the gym bag on the bed.

"No needles. Not even sticky tape." Talia shook her head. "Men can be such crybabies."

"I got stung once today. That's quite enough." Kyle pulled a book out of his bag. Something about flowers. Orchids. How odd.

Talia checked that the clear hood was connected. "Stung? By a bee?"

"No. Just a thorn."

Talia patted the hood. "We use a state-of-the-art remote brain sensor." She pointed to a red button on the control arm of the bed. "When you are ready to sleep, just push this button. The hood will lower itself and begin monitoring the smallest electric impulses generated by your brain."

Kyle sat on the bed and propped up the pillows.

"Here." Talia pushed the arm button controlling the backrest and raised it for him. In her haste, she brushed his hand. The smooth, warm contact made her skin tingle and blood rushed through her body.

"Thanks." Kyle's gaze lingered on her face. Slowly, still staring at her, he leaned back and opened his book.

Embarrassed and excited at the same time, Talia smiled. "If you need anything, just ask...." She managed not to blush at his answering grin and rushed to the door. "Good night, Kyle."

Early the next morning, when Talia reached the clinic, she expected Kyle to be long gone. She turned to the plump nurse watching the monitors. "Can I see the printout for Kyle Dormant?"

"I'm afraid he's still asleep." The nurse moved aside to offer Talia a clear view of the monitor showing Kyle in his bed.

"That's odd."

"Now that you mention it, he's been in delta-wave cycle for several hours."

"Several hours?" Talia frowned. A full cycle of deep sleep

rarely lasted more than a hundred minutes. Definitely off the charts. "Anything else?"

"Everything else is normal."

Could Talia have found the explanation that had eluded her? No wonder Kyle experienced sleep paralysis. He probably awakened directly from delta state without the usual transitions of alpha, REM, and beta brain waves. This would make for an interesting study case. "I better wake him up or he'll be late for work."

"Go gently." The nurse offered a motherly smile.

Talia didn't need the warning. "Scaring him to death or giving him a heart attack is the last thing I want."

Intrigued, Talia knocked on the door and picked up the file from the door pocket. Receiving no answer, she entered, set the file on the small table, and opened the drapes to let in the morning sun.

Kyle didn't react or blink. He slept, very still, except for the barely noticeable rise of his chest upon each slow breath. He looked so peaceful, so handsome through the Plexiglas hood. The night's growth of beard gave him a roguish quality that made him even more attractive, like a movie star caught in sleeping abandon.

Talia lifted the Plexiglas hood. Hesitantly, she took his strong hand in hers and caressed his fingers. "Hey, wake up. You should be on your morning run."

She patted his hand to no avail. As much as she hated it, Talia would have to be more forceful. She shook his shoulder. No response. Finally, she slapped his cheeks. Still no reaction. Worried, she felt his forehead. No fever.

Pulling a small flashlight out of her coat's breast pocket, she lifted one eyelid and checked for pupil dilatation. Normal. She consulted the monitors. All vital signs registered normal. The brain activity indicated deep sleep, but Kyle wouldn't wake up. He hadn't mentioned this ever happening before.

Talia dialed the nursing station from the phone on the bedside table. "I need a complete blood workup on patient Dormant right away."

She went to the table, snatched the file and opened it,

scanning through the paperwork for Kyle's next of kin. His father. She pulled out her cell phone and dialed the number.

"Morning..." The male voice sounded sleepy.

"Mr. Dormant? Sorry if I woke you."

"That's all right. Who are you?" His voice had the same musical quality as Kyle's. "I'm Dr. Beauregard. Are you aware that your son Kyle signed up for a sleep study?" Talia motioned to the nurse at the door to enter the room.

The man at the end of the line yawned. "He mentioned it. Why?"

"Did he ever have problems waking up in the morning?" Talia kept an eye on Kyle, hoping he would react to the nurse's tourniquet or to the needle, but he didn't.

"Not Kyle." Mr. Dormant chuckled. "He was always the first one up as a child, and he hasn't changed a bit."

"Does he have any medical condition that requires medications?" The forms said no, but sometime people lied.

"Not that I know of. Why don't you ask him?"

"That's the problem." Talia hesitated before spitting the ugly truth. "I can't. He won't wake up."

"What do you mean, won't?" The man took a noisy breath. "What did you do to my son?"

"Nothing." Talia hated the defensive tone in her voice. "He was just under observation."

"So what went wrong?"

"According to our instruments, he's just asleep. We have no explanation as to why he won't wake up. Does he take sleeping pills?" Talia's file said he didn't.

"I doubt it very much." A loud clatter at the other end of the line... then a pause.

"Sir? Are you all right?"

"I'm fine. Just dropped the damned phone," the man mumbled. "Where is my son? I want to see him."

After giving Mr. Dormant directions, Talia pocketed her phone and turned to the nurse. "I want a complete toxicology screen, and an emergency brain scan." Talia had to cover all the angles. She didn't want to miss anything.

The nurse nodded and left the room.

Spotting the gym bag on the floor, Talia set it on the table. She wasn't being nosey, just trying to help Kyle. She pulled out more books about orchids, designer underwear and a change of clothes, keys, and a cell phone. The shaving kit revealed men's cologne—Aqua de Gio. She smelled the cap and recognized last night's fragrance, sweet, masculine, and so seductive, just like Kyle.

She found no drugs or pills. Not even vitamins. To make absolutely sure, Talia checked the bathroom and the waste basket for empty alcohol bottles or pill wrappings, to no avail.

What could be the matter with Kyle? Had he taken something at home before coming to the clinic?

Back in her office, Talia hid from Kyle's father, who demanded to see her. She wanted to have something concrete to report.

When the preliminary blood work came back negative, Talia's confusion increased. She consulted eminent colleagues but they had no clue. The brain scan also came back negative. Kyle seemed perfectly healthy.

With some apprehension, Talia braced herself to face Kyle's father, who had taken watch in his son's room.

As she entered, the man walked up to her, worry creasing the lines on his noble brow. "What's wrong with my son? Why isn't he waking up?"

"We still don't know, sir." Talia moved to the other side of the bed, dreading the wrath of a loving father.

"What are you doing about it?"

"I've done everything I could so far, sir. We started an IV to make sure he doesn't get dehydrated and keeps up his strength. Until we know more about what caused this, we can only keep him under observation."

"Observation?" Mr. Dormant's face grew red and congested. "Excuse me, young lady, but I demand a second opinion."

"I understand, sir." Talia barely managed to keep her voice calm. "My colleagues concur, but you are welcome to contact any other expert."

"Believe me, I will." Mr. Dormant gestured toward his son.

"How long is he going to sleep? Hours? Days?"

"I cannot say... He could wake up any moment." Talia felt responsible. It happened on her watch.

Mr. Dormant looked confused. He straightened his spine, as if ashamed to be seen in that state. "Well, if there is nothing physically wrong with him, and you can't do anything, does he need to stay here? I'd rather have him at the villa. I can arrange for someone to take care of him at home."

"That's your privilege, sir." Talia would prefer to keep Kyle close, but she couldn't interfere. The patient wasn't under any treatment that required hospitalization. "I will need to visit him regularly to monitor his progress. And if there is any change for the worse, he'll have to be hospitalized, of course."

The days passed and each evening after work, Talia stopped at the Dormant villa on her way home. The imposing Tuscan residence resembled a stone castle with its round towers and arched windows. Tall junipers, flagstone courtyards, and gurgling fountains added to the medieval feel. At night, on a backdrop of stars, the amber lighting on the stone facade and the surrounding vegetation gave the villa a fairytale atmosphere.

As the attending physician, Talia had the run of Kyle's apartments in the Western tower. After making his report, the male nurse usually left for the night and Talia took over. She'd insisted the bank of monitors and the remote brain sensor be brought into Kyle's blue velvet room. Any change, for the worse or for the better, would immediately trigger Talia's pager. She'd made saving Kyle her life's mission.

Talia had explored Kyle's home office, hoping to find something helpful. His laptop revealed work related files, and a personal journal where Kyle talked about work, his dreams and visions, his episodes as he called them. He nurtured a few friends, had placed in marathons across the country, and spoke passionately about cats and orchids.

His last entry told her how he'd enjoyed their meeting and was looking forward to knowing her better. He even mentioned that since he'd seen her in his vision that morning,

Talia could be the one. The one? Premonition nonsense...

She envied the male nurse who bathed and shave Kyle each day. But on these long winter evenings, Kyle belonged to Talia. She spoke to him about her concerns, her small victories, her sadness at his condition. She petted the little Siamese eager for affection, or she read aloud from the orchid books. Sometimes Talia just sat there, watching Kyle sleep. Often, she dozed off in the chair.

Just off the plush bedroom, a large balcony had been transformed into a greenhouse. A sophisticated automated system kept an even temperature and humidity in the glass room, shielded from the Arizona sun by movable white screens that lowered as soon as the sun hit the glass pane. Watering also was automated, but the orchids still needed care.

Having learned from the books she read to Kyle, Talia decided to try her hand at horticulture. Using the small clippers and tools left on the work table, she nipped a dead leaf here, adjusted a stake there, retied a stem, misted the leaves. This hobby soothed and relaxed her. It also made her feel closer to Kyle.

Caught between a dream and a nightmare, Kyle remained paralyzed in bed, mute but fully aware, his consciousness free to roam as he enjoyed the reassuring presence of Dr. Talia Beauregard. He couldn't believe the woman he hungered for had come to him and nurtured with love his beloved cat and his precious orchids.

He wanted to tell her how he felt, and who had caused his condition. By now, Kyle had figured it out. Although he wasn't sure how the poison worked, he knew Uncle Gerald had found a way to get rid of him with impunity.

Split between heaven and hell, Kyle wanted to take Talia in his arms. But for the remainder of his sleeping life, he would burn for a kiss that might never come...

Talia admired the most beautiful orchid in Kyle's greenhouse, a tall plant with a large white flower, scalloped petals, and a pink spotted heart. The label on the pot said "Sleeping Beauty." The name struck a chord of morbid humor in Talia's mind. The provenance of the plant indicated the country of Bhutan. How exotic.

Carefully pushing aside the petals, Talia noticed a thorn just under the heart. None of Kyle's books mentioned such things on orchids. Then she remembered Kyle mentioning he'd pricked himself on a thorn the night he came to the clinic. Could this be the source of Kyle's predicament?

Heart pounding, Talia placed the globe atop the plant. Carrying her precious loot, she left the villa in a hurry, careful not to be seen by the help. Then she drove off into the night.

Calling in a favor, Talia arranged to have Curie-Prentis Labs open for an emergency. She set the rare plant on the black counter in front of the bleary-eyed chemist. "I want a full analysis on whatever is on the thorn of this plant. Be careful. I suspect poison."

The nerdy employee slapped a biohazard sticker on the plastic globe then glanced at Talia above gold-rimmed glasses. "When do you need it?"

"Three weeks ago. I have a patient in a coma."

The lab results seemed to take forever, but Talia finally received the call.

"You were right. The mass spectrophotometer found traces of quiescence hydrochloride. Fortunately for your patient, there is an antidote."

The rare chemical occurred naturally in Bhutan and its surrounding countries. A freak of nature. The blood work didn't find it because it lay below the chemical radar. But someone had brought this forbidden plant from Bhutan, and that someone would pay for the crime.

Talia remembered the last entry in Kyle's journal. A boardroom brawl over the return of a long exiled uncle. And how the man apologized by giving Kyle a rare orchid. Wasn't he returning from Bhutan? It all made sense.

After ordering the antidote, Talia called Kyle's father.

Arrested the same day, Gerald grinned to the cameras on the five o'clock news. He offered no excuse, no regrets to the journalists' questions. He looked proud of himself. He'd gambled for the control of the company and lost. To him, this was just another gamble, a risky adventure worth a try. He had no shame about what he had done to his nephew. How despicable.

❧

Talia had Kyle brought to the hospital for the administration of the antidote. The procedure could trigger unexpected adverse reactions. Worst scenario, Kyle might die. But Talia couldn't stand seeing him in such a predicament, and this was his only chance to regain consciousness. If it failed... but Talia didn't want to think about a negative outcome.

In the hospital room, under the stare of concerned friends and relatives, Talia injected the antidote into Kyle's IV drip and prayed the clear liquid would bring Kyle back. Prayed? How long had it been since she prayed?

Watching these expectant faces, Talia felt the weight of Kyle's life on her shoulders. Did they think she was some kind of god? She only did what she could. And if it weren't enough, Kyle would pay the ultimate price.

Time slowed to the rhythm of the lazy drip of antidote, drop by minuscule drop, into the clear IV tube.

Talia desperately held on to the hope that she and Kyle were meant for each other. And if they had a predestined future, he had to be alive for it. Even in her mind, she sounded like a weirdo, but she couldn't help it. She needed Kyle... alive.

Talia's heart beat faster when the monitors above the bed displayed a different type of brain waves. "Yes! He is reacting!"

First rapid eye movements gave her hope. Kyle moved one finger, one arm, one foot. He had tremors, like during a nightmare. But at least it was the beginning of a reaction.

When his heart rate accelerated beyond normal rhythm, and his body shook uncontrollably, Talia realized he was going into seizure. "Every visitor out of the room. Now!"

"I need help here!" Talia shouted to the nurses, while restraining Kyle, whose jerky movements endangered his own safety.

Nurses ran to Kyle's bedside. Talia watched, helpless, as the monitors showed life signs far beyond acceptable limits.

Had she given Kyle too much antidote? Not enough? Dear God!

Despite the sedative and anticonvulsants, Kyle kept shaking. Finally, he calmed down and lay inert, spent. His heart rate slowed gradually. Talia dared to hope, but the heart rate kept slowing dangerously despite Talia's best care. Then it was no more. The flat line beep of the machines indicated clinical death.

Stunned, Talia realized she'd killed Kyle. She couldn't accept that.

"Crash cart, now!" She snatched the paddles and rubbed them together. "Clear!"

The first shock didn't bring Kyle back.

"Clear!" The second shock didn't seem to work either, but before she could administer one more, the beep of the heart monitor resumed, slow at first, then accelerating to a near-normal rate. Relief washed over Tania and she couldn't help the tears flowing down her face. "Thank you, God!"

But Kyle still slept. His brain waves indicated a normal sleep pattern. Why didn't he wake up?

"Leave me alone with him."

After the nurses left, Talia bent over Kyle, so close to his handsome face. How she wanted to kiss him! Before she even realized it, her lips were on his, soft and warm, and she tasted his mouth. Licorice. A sweet, dark taste. To her surprise, he responded to her kiss, and his deep brown eyes opened.

Talia stepped back, overjoyed and amazed. "It worked."

Kyle smiled and winked. "I thought you'd never wake me with that kiss."

"What kiss?" Hot shame flushed Talia's face.

"Don't be coy. I know everything."

"In that case…" She brought her lips close to his.

Kyle took her mouth eagerly, his strong arms pulling her against him on the bed.

Talia's euphoria made her forget the hospital room. She savored his strength, his possessive embrace. His kiss was soft and strong, just like she had dreamed it would be.

"I told you we were meant for each other," he whispered in

her ear. "And I'm going to need many more of these kisses to ensure my full recovery."

"As your healer, it is my sworn duty to comply," she whispered back and claimed his lips once again.

The End

Born in France, award-winning author Vijaya Schartz never conformed to anything. She traveled the world and brings an exotic quality to her writing. Her romantic novels, contemporary or futuristic, are filled with action and collected many five-star reviews. Reviewers dubbed them exciting and compared them to Indiana Jones movies, Battlestar Galactica, X-files, and Stargate. Vijaya loves cats and has a cat in each and every story, although sometimes it's a predator, or an alien monster cat. She presently lives in sunny Arizona.

Visit her website at: www.vijayaschartz.com

Immerse Yourself in Fantasy

with

Decadent Publishing

&

www.decadentpublishing.com

A Note from the Publisher:

When Amanda McIntyre first approached me about doing a Faery Anthology to benefit Tina Gerow, I was delighted. Not only is Tina one of my Sister Fae, but as a former critical care nurse, my experience working at Harborview Medical Center in the Neuro ICU provided knowledge of the life-altering challenges – physical, emotional and financial, that Tina and her family faced. Decadent Publishing is honored to be a part of this project and we sincerely hope you enjoyed these fabulous stories.

~Lisa Omstead

9 781936 394685